Titles available in the Jack Hunter series
(in reading order)

Jack Hunter
Secret of the King

Jack Hunter
The French Connection

Coming in 2013
The third instalment in the riveting
'Jack Hunter' adventure series.

Jack Hunter
Legend of the Two Giants

THE WORLD'S FIRST  INTERACTIVE BOOK

 brings you a book unlike any other. Not only can you
read the adventure, but you can play the adventure

Within the pages of this book are pictures,
special markers, to unlock a 3D adventure game.

Watch the action come alive as the game leaps out
of the pages in interactive 3D.

This is not just a book, this is an

IT'S A BOOK ... IT'S A GAME ... IT'S 3D ... IT'S AN

COMING JANUARY 1ST 2013

Jack Hunter App
http://ibolive.com/jackapp

Immerse yourself in a world beyond a world.
Not only can you read about Jack and his friends
embarking on their new adventure but, now you can join
them with your very own adventure game – in 3D!
Download the **Jack Hunter App**
and be sent back over six hundred years in time.
The esoteric order known as the *Four Corners* have hidden
a special parchment. To keep this powerful secret hidden
from the rest of mankind the *Four Corners* have divided
the ancient scroll and placed the pieces in four separate
locations hidden within their castle stronghold.
***Can you piece the parchment together and unravel
the world's greatest secret?***
Part 1 will be available to download on **Android** and **IOS**
devices **01/01/2013**.

Find the clues, unlock the secret, solve the mystery and
discover the treasure.

Dedication

Raven Jade Addy-Cruz 1989 – 2012.
Too soon

Special mentions

Russell (PIXEL tweaks) Holden – fantastic cover design
Pete (the pen) Langley – superb illustrations
Michael (bright spark) Ford – pure awesomeness

And for everyone else who believed and supported me
– you know who you are!

JACK HUNTER
The French Connection

by
Martin King

First published in Great Britain 2012 by RAZOR SHARP

Digital copyright © 2012 Martin King

A CIP catalogue record for this book is available from the British Library.

Printed and bound in the UK & US
ISBN 978 0 9571 0211 8

RAZOR SHARP BOOKS

Introduction

This book contains numbers in the form of an Ottendorf cipher. By unlocking the cipher you will be able to uncover the location of a secret door. Accept the challenge and help Jack unlock the door to discover what lies beyond.

Crack the code

Unlock the hidden door

Finish the puzzle

Find the secret chapter

The Adventure Continues...

Chapter One

Jack lay awake... there was something important he needed to remember. A nagging thought erupted into realisation. Suddenly remembering, he sat bolt upright. Today was the beginning of the best week, ever.

Normally, he would hit the snooze button at least three times until his mum finally came and banged on his bedroom door. Not this morning! Cheering loudly, he leapt from the security of his bed with a grin of excitement beaming across his face.

"JAAACK!" his mum yelled from downstairs as he opened the bedroom door.

Jack was determined nothing would ruin his day – not even a run-in with The Stoneman could not dampen his spirits. David Pullen, nicknamed 'The Stoneman', was the top of Jack's most hated person list. In fact, he was the *only* person Jack did not like. The Stonemans' favourite pastime seemed to consist of making his life a misery and Jack did not have a clue why.

"Make sure you get some breakfast," his mum called.

"Al-mmm-right," he replied with a mouth full of foaming, white toothpaste. As he waved his fancy new electric toothbrush around, toothpaste splattered the bathroom, covering the mirror. The toothpaste went everywhere except where it was supposed to.

"Jack, are you cleaning your teeth?" his mum asked

outside the bathroom door. Caught by surprise, Jack dropped his toothbrush into the basin. The battery-powered bristles continued to whirl, splashing the gooey, pearly white substance all over his face and dark navy school sweatshirt.

If his mum could hear him cleaning his teeth then what was the point of asking the question? It was obvious he would not be able to reply. Jack argued his case to the person staring back at him from the streaked mirror. The boy with white foaming lips and snow-covered top stared back. After skilfully preparing his defence, "Yeah," was all Jack could muster.

"Why are you cleaning them now? You're supposed to clean them *after* your breakfast," his mum continued. "Otherwise there's no point in cleaning them at all."

Jack could not believe what he was hearing. His parents were always telling him to make sure he brushed his teeth. The very morning he actually did clean them, somehow, he was still scolded.

A loud knock at the front door interrupted the victory speech he was now preparing. Jack was certain he would come home triumphant. He hastily sponged the splash marks off his school top guessing his friend had arrived. Holly was sort of Jack's best friend – sort of, because that privilege was shared with three others.

A little over eight months ago Jack was cruelly ripped from everything he knew and dragged to Barnoldswick, a sleepy town in Lancashire. It seemed at that moment his life was at an end. According to all the statistics, data, and percentages, Jack's life should have been duller than a big, fat, RUBBISH!

That is until he met Holly (real name Shaun), Martin and Jules Brown – who lived next door – and BT. If you could somehow squash the four of them together, then Jack would have the perfect best friend all rolled into one.

The events of those school holidays would never be forgotten! Just a few weeks after moving to Northern England Jack became something of a local celebrity. Every newspaper wanted to have his picture on the front page. It meant those first few weeks at his new school which would normally have been a living nightmare were in fact, brilliant. Everyone wanted to be his friend.

That was nearly nine months ago. Next week was the Easter holidays. Jack was going on holiday to Disneyland in Paris with his best friends. It was going to be his best holiday ever.

Jack had never been abroad before. The furthest he had ever travelled was Anglesey, a small island off the coast of Wales. Two fantastic weeks stretched before him, starting that afternoon with a trip to Burnley.

Today, out of his four best friends, only Holly would be walking with him on the one-and-a-quarter mile trek to school. Jules and Martin were both staying home with a case of the chickenpox, and BT would not be eleven for another six months, he still went to Coates Lane

Primary School. A smile briefly spread across Jack's face at the thought of Martin missing the BIG day, if only because Martin could be so annoying at times with his childish pranks.

Jack rushed down stairs to the front door.

"Have you got everything, mate?" the super-organised Holly asked, casually leaning against the doorframe and swinging his foot at an imaginary football, while holding his school bag in one hand and the remains of a chocolate-coated Pop Tart in the other.

Jack frowned.

"And, do you have your money for the trip?" reminded Holly, before polishing off the last piece of his breakfast. Holly eagerly licked his fingers clean removing all traces of food.

"Make sure you've got everything, Jack," his mum's voice was still ringing loudly in his ears as he was about to step out of the house. "And don't forget to take some bananas, darling. They're good for giving you energy." Jack was beginning to feel dizzier than a spinning top. If only everyone would just stop talking all at once.

MONEY! The word struck an immediate cord with him.

"Murrrm," said Jack, stepping back into the house and throwing her one of his puppy-dog-eyed looks. "Can I have a tenner? I need it for the school trip." Before his mum had chance to reply, he added, "plerr-ease," just for good measure.

"I'm sorry, love. I spent it all on shopping yesterday. I needed to get the food for our holiday. You'd better check with your dad. I'm sure he'll have some money in his wallet."

That was all Jack needed. His dad's wallet was more secure than Fort Knox with Scrooge in charge of the keys. Not holding out much hope he entered the kitchen. At that time in the morning, it was the lair of his ferocious dad. He dragged a reluctant Holly along, reasoning; "It'll be more difficult for Dad to refuse giving the money to me, if you're there. Besides, he's always saying how much I should be more like you."

His dad sat at the table with a mug of tea and a plate of toast. Roger Hunter enjoyed reading the paper, but most of all he enjoyed circling all the errors he found with a red felt marker. "Hello Jacky," he greeted his son without looking up. "Shouldn't you be on your way to school by now?" he asked in his usual annoying manner. "Oh, hello there, Shaun," momentarily glancing up, he greeted Holly as he circled another mistake in the paper. "Did you know that on average there are one hundred and thirty seven grammatical errors in every newspaper?"

Holly shook his head.

"Now there's a saying; if a job's worth doing, then do it well! Wouldn't you agree?"

Holly nodded in agreement.

"Anyway, you make sure our Jacky doesn't lead you astray." Roger Hunter laughed at his own quip. His dad's efforts to impress Holly were somewhat curtailed by a blob of strawberry jam rolling down his chin.

Jack wanted to shout at his dad. A vision of red Indians tying his dad to the chair while the chief wrote JACK on his father's forehead in buffalo poo to remind him his son's name was Jack, quickly vanished as he remembered the mission. "Dad… I was wondering if I could have, erm, a tenner for my school trip…it's today? Please…" he asked shuffling his feet on the spot. "It's really important."

Lifting his head out of the newspaper, "They call me Sam Dilly, not Damn Silly," his dad laughed.

Slamming the front door as he left the house Jack jumped outside with one giant leap. He hated the way his dad showed off in front of his friends. His dad's stupid expression was still rattling around in his head. The glorious, crystal blue skies of the previous days were somewhat tainted by a mugginess that told him a storm loomed. Torrential rain would completely spoil the big day.

The two boys were no more than five minutes into their hike to school when Jack heard a faint voice cry, "Jack! Holly!" Jack spun around. There was no one to be seen.

"Did you hear someone shout us?" Jack asked Holly.

"Look, is that… BT?" Holly pointed to someone who looked more like a one-foot-tall garden gnome, since they were so far away. BT was not particularly short; he just appeared smaller than his friends did because he was only ten years old.

Jack waved and turned back around. There was no time to waste. Old Crumble had made it perfectly clear that anyone late that week, even once, would be dropped from the team – and he was not going to allow anything to stop him. Jack had not even placed one foot in front of the other when he felt a whooshing sensation by his side. Before he knew what was happening, someone had snatched his school bag.

Jack looked up just in time to see BT whizzing past, red and orange sparks spewing out from his heels. "Turbo shoes!" BT cheered with a huge grin, victoriously waving Jack's bag in the air.

Speechless, Jack turned to Holly for some kind of explanation. Holly just returned Jack's blank expression.

"Look out!" shouted Jack. BT was too busy looking at them and not in the direction he was heading. Before he could slow down, he hit a low wall. Everything happened so fast. Jack and Holly remained rooted to the spot. BT tumbled backwards over the wall, disappearing out of sight, still clutching Jack's school bag.

SPLASH!

BT had fallen into the canal!

Chapter Two

Jack stood still, mouth wide open. The full impact of what he had just witnessed slowly sinking in. As if that wasn't bad enough, he knew BT hated water – BT could not swim.

"Quick!" shouted Holly, already rushing to help BT.

Snapping into action, Jack raced towards his friend. Reaching the canal bridge at the same moment as Holly, Jack peered over the edge. BT was nowhere to be seen. Then the water gurgled like a plughole with bubbles rippling on the surface. They both ran down the steps that led to the canal towpath, just as BT's head resurfaced.

"Heeelllp!" he squealed, "I-I can't swiiim!" His head bobbing under the surface of the water once again.

Without hesitation, Jack threw off his coat before jumping into the canal. The shock from the icy cold water was instant. His whole body went into an immediate spasm as his muscles locked. At the same time his throat began to burn as he swallowed more frogspawn flavoured murky water. He was struggling to breathe. For a second, all he wanted to do was close his eyes. To dream about lying on a hot, sunny beach, cool waves lapping at his feet.

Holly's voice broke through his consciousness. Instinctively, Jack knew what to do. Taking a deep breath and frantically kicking his feet, he swam into the middle of the canal to the spot he last remembered seeing BT.

Taking a deep breath, Jack dove under the water. Opening his eyes he instantly wished he hadn't, they stung as though he was swimming through acid. Ignoring the burning sensation, he tried to search through the murky depths, but there was no sign of BT.

Jack's lungs were beginning to ache. He returned to the surface gasping for air. Suddenly, he felt his leg kick against something. Taking another deep breath he went back under.

He opened his eyes and again they began to sting. All he was interested in was finding his friend, getting BT to safety. BT was barely moving. Pushing through the pain barrier, Jack fought his way through the murky water.

Jack needed to act fast. BT was drifting further away. With another kick of his feet, Jack lunged for BT again. Finally, he grabbed hold of his friend. With every ounce of strength remaining, he propelled them towards the safety of dry land.

Seconds later, Jack pulled a gasping, wet, and bedraggled BT to the banking. Reaching down, Holly helped pull the pair of them out of the water and onto the canal towpath. BT was somehow still clutching the school bag he had swiped from Jack earlier.

Out of breath, late for school, and his uniform ruined, Jack miserably slumped to the ground on the canal towpath. He had been looking forward to this day for almost a month. Today was the Lancashire

School's Cup final. Not only was playing in the cup final supposed to be the highlight of Jack's year, but it meant he would get to miss the afternoon class as well. That was inconsequential now as his friend lay with his eyes closed, deathly quiet.

"What do we do now?" asked Jack, a slight quiver in his voice.

"I don't know. I think you need to give him the kiss of life," shrugged Holly, as if it seemed the most natural suggestion in the world.

"You've gotta be kidding me!" exclaimed Jack. "There's no way I'm giving him a kiss."

"You'll have to, mate," urged Holly.

"What do you mean, 'I have to?'" asked Jack. "Why me? Why not you?" he demanded.

"Because you're already contaminated with canal water," said Holly with irritating logic.

"So…?" said Jack. Nothing about his day was going according to plan.

"Yeah, well…you're the nearest to him and besides, if you don't hurry up, he'll die. Look…he's not moving!"

"But I-I, er," Jack lamely argued. He had no intention of kissing a boy. But, he definitely did not want BT to die. The thought of being the cause of his friend's death because he refused to give him mouth to mouth resuscitation was unbearable. Closing his eyes, he slowly moved in until he hovered inches from BT's face. The way Jack hesitated was as though BT carried a deadly virus.

"Hurry up," urged Holly.

"That's easy for you to say," retorted Jack, "You're not the one who has to do it."

"Just close your eyes and pucker up," said Holly, trying hard not to smirk.

Sticking his lips out, Jack closed his eyes and reluctantly moved even closer in an attempt to save his friend's life.

Suddenly, BT opened his eyes. "What're you doing? Are you trying to kiss me?" he shrieked.

"Er-rrrrr, NO!" stammered Jack.

"You was…!"

"Honestly, I wasn't," protested Jack.

"Ha-ha, had you going there, mate," laughed Holly with BT joining in.

"What're you both laughing at?" snarled Jack.

"I was awake the whole time," said BT, shivering cold, but roaring with laughter.

"That's not funny! I was trying to save your life!" yelled Jack, upset that no one appreciated his selfless act.

"Jack, look at the time! We need to hurry up. I've never been late for school once. Besides, remember what 'old Crumble' announced in assembly? Anyone late for school this week won't be allowed to go with the team," said Holly wiping away the memory of Jack's heroics.

Leaping to his feet quicker than a spawning salmon realisation hit Jack, his clothes were soaking wet. There was no way in the world he could get away with going to school looking like a drowned rat. His only option would be to go home and hope, by some miracle, his parents would both be out.

***

After the worst possible start, Jack's day began to improve. First, both his parents were nowhere to be seen and, a newly cleaned uniform hung neatly in his wardrobe. The shame was he only possessed one pair of school shoes and they were the ones he was wearing.

Morning bell had already rung by the time Holly and Jack entered through the main door. Everywhere was deathly quiet. The only audible sound came from the squishing of Jack's sodden shoes. Jack and Holly were nearly at the end of the corridor when The Stoneman walked round the corner.

He disliked The Stoneman. Ever since the day Jack had arrived in town, The Stoneman (Jack liked the thought The Stoneman's nickname came from the prehistoric era) had been on his case. He was your number one, premium, class A bully. Today, The Stoneman was not alone. His two sidekicks, Beefy and Pratt, were with him. Although they were both in the year above The Stoneman, they always seemed to follow him around like sheep behind a shepherd.

"Look at who we have here," said The Stoneman, an unnerving grin spreading across his hideous face.

"Hunter," replied Beefy excitedly, looking pleased he had got the question right.

"Hunter-Duncer..." added Pratt. He always did that. Jack never understood why. Perhaps Pratt thought it made him sound intelligent when he added a rhyming word at the end of everything he said. Someone needed to tell Pratt that Hunter and Duncer didn't even rhyme.

"And Holly 'my-poor-uncle...boo-hoo' Hollingsworth," laughed The Stoneman.

Jack glanced at Holly and threw him a look as if to say, "I'm sorry! Please ignore him." But Holly did not notice Jack's efforts. He just stood there silently like he was in some sort of trance.

Jack felt awful. Ever since things went weird with his uncle, Holly had been different. That morning, when they were laughing down by the canal, it was like the real Holly was back. Lately, Holly would disappear into his books like some kind of recluse – sometimes for weeks on end. Not once had Holly spoken about what happened to his uncle that fateful day back in the summer holidays. It was the one thing that left a sour taste on the otherwise momentous discovery. Martin did try on one occasion to talk about it and ended up with a punch in the belly. They never mentioned it again.

"We're late for class..." pleaded Jack, more interested in saving Holly from another verbal assault about his uncle than what might happen to him. "So you'll have to let us go."

"Why? So you and Holly cry-boy can go boo-hooing to the teacher!" laughed The Stoneman, rubbing his fists against his eyes with Beefy and Pratt cutting off their retreat. They were surrounded.

Annoyingly, teachers were always around, until the one time you actually needed their help. Right at that moment, not a single teacher was in sight. Without mercy, The Stoneman pushed Jack hard. He flew past the rather tubby Beefy, slamming backwards into the wall.

"Oof," groaned Jack, the wind knocked out of him. "I've got the cup match this aft'. If you give me an injury, I won't be able to play and we might lose." Out of breath Jack leaned against the wall quite proud of his remark. After all, surely they wanted their own school to win.

"Don't care 'bout football," replied The Stoneman.

"We don't?" said Beefy. Both he and Pratt's expressions told Jack they did not agree.

Just then, a delayed message in Jack's brain alerted him to a new problem. The Stoneman had jabbed Jack with his knee, giving him the biggest, hardest dead leg imaginable. The pain was excruciating!

Without explanation, the three bullies scampered back around the corner. Relieved, Jack collapsed against the wall. As Holly rushed to his aid, a thunderous voice shattered through the temporary reprieve.

"HUNTER! HOLLINGSWORTH!" shouted Mr. McIntyre in his faded Scottish accent. Any visions of lifting the trophy vanished quicker than a puff of smoke. Mr. McIntyre took great pleasure inflicting misery on the pupils. It was as though, when he was a child, aliens had come down to earth and, for some weird experiment, sucked all the fun out of his body. Now, both Jack and Holly were about to reap the rewards of that freak encounter.

"My, my, my! What have we here?!" grinned Mr. McIntyre. "I'm surprised to see you, Hollingsworth. Not like you to be out of lesson, breaking the rules." Holly remained silent.

"And you, Hunter! Aren't you supposed to be having the honour of representing our school in the prestigious Lancashire Cup final this afternoon? And wasn't one of the requisites laid out by Mr. Rumble that anyone on the team not following protocol would NOT be attending the match?" The sneer in his voice made Jack's hopes plummet.

"I–" protested Jack.

"I haven't finished yet, mi-laddo! Why, in my day, you would have been clapped in irons for less. Look at the state of you! Let's see what Mr. Rumble thinks about your slovenly behaviour and disagreeable appearance."

Being dragged to the headmaster's office meant only one thing. Jack would without doubt not be allowed to play. He was going to miss the cup final!

Chapter Three

Mr. Rumble, the headmaster, whom everyone called Crumble was tall and thin like a stick of rhubarb with spiky hair. He was nothing like how Jack pictured a headmaster should look. His clothes hung on him as though he had been dragged through a hedge backwards and his tie looked like it had been tied by a two-year-old. Crumble sat silently behind his desk, the calm before the storm.

Jack felt bad for Holly. When it came to study, Holly was like a pre-programmed robot from another planet with instructions to learn as much as possible. He had never known a kid who liked school more. They both sat in Crumble's office receiving a lecture, the headmaster continued talking ... and talking.

"It is becoming rather apparent," Crumble was still rambling on, fifteen minutes later, "that you obviously have a lack of respect for authority. Instead of falling in line with the rest of civilised society, you appear hell bent on wanton destruction and..." Went on ... and on ... and on!

Jack's face was dutifully paying attention, but his mind was elsewhere. A photograph in a dark wooden frame sat on the head teacher's desk, just about visible above a mountain of disorganised papers. A younger looking Crumble sporting a very unfashionable v-neck tank top stood towering at the side of a pretty woman, a young boy stood in front of them. Jack found it hard to believe that someone as miserable as Crumble could ever have a son. The boy was the double of the headmaster.

Crumble sat twiddling his fountain pen backwards and forwards between his fingers, in a repetitive motion that was beginning to drive Jack bonkers. Twenty-seven minutes and thirty-two seconds later, Jack duly noted, the lecture was over. Finally, Crumble delivered the verdict. Detention! It was so harsh, especially since both he and Holly had just saved someone's life and been bullied by The Stoneman. There was no justice!

***

"Shussh!" spat Megan.

Mathematics was not Jack's best subject. It tied with history, geography, science and English for his least favourite lesson. Jack was sitting next to Megan Wilpear, who happened to be one of twins. This was really peculiar in Jack's opinion because they looked nothing alike. For one, Megan's hair was bright red. Meanwhile, Monica, her twin sister, was pasty white with bushy brown hair that had a tendency to stick out in every direction. Jack did not know anyone with as much hair as Megan. The masses of curly, red hair covered half of her face, which was full of freckles.

Jack threw his rubber and hit Holly on the shoulder. Holly turned around sharply a thunderous glare on his face. "I'm sorry," whispered Jack, trying to avoid the

17

attentions of Miss. Turnbull, who was busy writing square roots on the board.

"Sorry? I've never been so humiliated in all my life," replied Holly hotly. "I've never, EVER, been late for school or even–"

"Shaun Hollingsworth!"

"Er, yes, Miss?"

"Are you paying attention?"

"Of course, Miss?" replied Holly sounding hurt at the mere hint she doubted his integrity.

"Then, can you tell me, what is the square root of minus one?"

"Erm, one...no, erm...I think...minus one divided by itself equals," he half muttered. "Minus one, Miss...?"

"See me after class," she barked, followed by a subdued ripple of laughter throughout the room.

Jack felt awful. All he wanted to do was make amends and that was despite his own problems. Still smarting from receiving detention from crusty old Crumble ... his thigh muscle ached from The Stoneman kneeing him ... his feet were cold and soggy from his wet shoes ... even his toes were going all crinkly. Now, on top of all that, Holly was giving him the silent treatment.

Originally, Jack thought it was hilarious that Martin would be missing the big match. It wasn't until he was sitting in Crumble's office with the thought of not going himself that Jack realised how gutted Martin must feel. He made a mental note to make it up somehow. Jack had still been allowed to go to Burnley for the cup final – luckily because a few of the football team's key players had been struck down with chickenpox, Martin included.

Square roots were not for Jack. He had more important things on his mind and he stared dreamily out of the window. Behind the school was a large football pitch that sloped away. Beyond the pitch was a field and further in the distance, you could just about see the canal.

At the bottom of the school grounds at the far end of the football pitch stood a tall person sporting an unusually long robe, their face hidden behind a dark hood. Jack quickly checked to see that Miss. Turnbull was still busy, preoccupied writing something on the whiteboard, before turning back around and peering through the window again. He blinked hard twice. The figure was still there. He knew it had not been his imagination. Ever since the night he had discovered the treasure, Jack was positive he was being stalked.

The stranger raised their arm seemingly pointing straight at Jack. He instinctively ducked under his desk. With an ear-splitting screech Jack accidently pushed his chair too hard, sending the chair flying backwards. He fell with a thud onto the wooden floor.

"JACK HUNTER!" shouted Miss. Turnbull. "I believe you're already skating on thin ice as it is. Do you want to go to Burnley this afternoon? And as the team Captain I expected better." Sheepishly, Jack nodded while retrieving his chair. "Because it appears to me *your* destiny lies elsewhere. Anymore shenanigans and you'll be staying behind and catching up with your arithmetic."

Dragging his chair back to his desk and sitting down, Jack sat upright. Miss. Turnbull frowned at him. That was it; Jack was determined to be on his double-best behaviour. He wasn't going to do anything that could jeopardise his one opportunity of playing in the big match.

***

After the tedious group hug to the backdrop of the blackening sky and the usual *Braveheart* battle speech by Mr. Senior, one of the games teachers, Jack went to sit down. He could not believe he was being benched – if you could call the mound of grass he had to sit on at the side of the pitch, a bench. And he was supposed to be the team captain!

Mr. Senior sporting an electric blue tracksuit had noticed Jack limping, although Jack protested he was fine. The insignificant bruise on his thigh was only the size of a tennis ball, so he could have easily played. The game kicked off. Jack was still feeling sorry for himself when the other team sprang the offside trap. It was two against one. Smitho was trying to get back to defend the goal but looked like he was not going to make it. The lanky, blond-haired kid from Burnley Bankside unleashed a fierce shot. Jack gasped as the ball flew past Ryan in goal. To his relief, the ball clipped the top of the crossbar and went over the top.

Jack felt a tiny droplet on the end of his nose and as he looked around to see who was messing about, the heaven's opened. The torrential downpour only lasted ten minutes, but it was enough to soak Jack through for the second time that day. He sat on the small mound of grass soaking wet, freezing cold and feeling miserable.

If only Mr. Senior would let Jack play, they would have a much better chance of winning. Bankside were unbeaten in something like *fifty* games! The last time the two teams had met in a league match earlier in the year, his school had been murdered 5 - 0. Jack had been looking forward to today. It was a chance to gain revenge for that mauling and he had dreamt about scoring the winning goal at least a thousand times.

The halftime whistle blew.

The game was scoreless. There was still an opportunity for Jack to play in the game. During the break, he attempted running up and down the touchline to get Mr. Senior's attention. If he could impress the games teacher and show he was fit, he might get to play for the whole second half. Unfortunately, Mr. Senior did not even notice him.

It was turning into a disaster for Jack. The second half kicked-off. The day had promised so much and was supposed to end with Jack being the school hero.

Seventy minutes already gone.

Desperate to get in the game, Jack kept looking

across at Mr. Senior longingly. The secret was to attract his attention, let him know he was there, but without making it obvious. The teacher spent most of his time marching up and down the touchline and bellowing out instructions like, "Smith, get up that flank!" or "Clear it then, Robinson!" and Jack's personal favourite, but solely because it was aimed at the player keeping him out of the game: "Shoot, you idiot...Doh!" Mr. Senior collapsed in despair, his face buried in his hands. Just like Jack, Mr. Senior hated losing.

Seventy-five minutes on the clock.

The score-line was still goalless. Jack could barely watch a single kick. Only when the noise from the screaming crowd rose to a level that broke through his consciousness did Jack turn his attention toward the game.

Eighty-three minutes.

"You're on..." Mr. Senior suddenly called over to the bench. Jack's ears pricked up. There was only about six minutes of normal time to play. A boy with long, gangly legs nicknamed Shorts, who lived at the opposite end of town, stood up. Jack's heart sank.

"Not you..." said Mr. Senior, shaking his head despairingly. "Come on, Hunter! Get a move on." The words did not register at first. His head was telling his feet to move, but they were frozen. Jack had waited eighty-four minutes to get the call, and when it finally came his feet would not react.

"Well Hunter…do you want to play or not?" demanded the teacher, standing with his hands on his hips.

For the next five minutes, Jack never got a touch of the ball. He ran like a lopsided chicken and the only thing that stopped Mr. Senior from noticing his lame effort was the poor state of the pitch. It was turning into a mud bath. Almost impossible to stand on your feet with two good legs, Jack was struggling by on one, The Stoneman's dead leg was having its desired effect.

Suddenly, the ball dropped at Jack's feet and probably more to do with luck than skill, taking into account the atrocious conditions, he went past the last defender. This was his chance, all he had to do was beat the goalie and he would have an open goal.

Just when his chance to be the hero presented itself, to score the winner in the last minute that would see them lift the Lancashire Cup, his studs got stuck in a divot. At the crucial moment, he lost his footing and stumbled. One minute he could have been the hero, the next he was flat on his face in the mud. He could already hear the laughter in his head.

The whistle blew. Full time.

Jack had blown his one chance.

The game was over.

Jack's teammates pulled him up out of the mud and started hugging him. He could hear cheering.

The referee had awarded a penalty.

"Penalty?" questioned Jack, he had only tripped.

Some of the Bankside players bumped him, nearly knocking him back into the swampy mire. "Cheat!" a kid with mud-covered spectacles shouted at him. As Jack turned round to defend himself, he saw a crowd of Bankside players surrounding the referee who miraculously did not have a single speck of mud on him.

"It's not a penalty," Jack explained to Smitho, the closest team mate to him. "I tripped. I have to tell the ref."

"Are you mad? You can't. Do you want every kid in school to hate you forever?"

"No, but–"

"No but, nothing! Besides, there's nothing you can do once the ref's made his decision. They're not allowed to change it... apparently FIFA rules or sommat like that…" Smitho explained convincingly.

The ball had already been placed on the spot. After all the commotion, this could possibly be the last kick of the match. Jack felt guilty. He stood staring at the ball, a concoction of mixed emotions floating around inside his head. He was no cheat. A voice from somewhere within told him to miss – on purpose.

Standing in front of the football, his innards felt like exploding. He had heard people describe the funny feeling inside your stomach as butterflies. Right then it felt more like a Rottweiler ripping his intestines to shreds.

Jack tried to block everything out. The uproar seemed to vanish from around him. The only thing that mattered was to bury the ball into the back of the net. Half-heartedly, he stepped up and pulled his right leg back. Normally, he would stare the goalie out, send him the wrong way. On this occasion, he could not even look him in the eye.

He struck the ball!

There was nothing more he could do. This was it. He had hit it hard and low. The ball flew towards the left-hand bottom corner. The goalie had guessed its trajectory, but the ball was too quick for him. As the goalkeeper went to ground with his hand outstretched, the ball had already shot past him.

Jack scrunched up his eyes. Slowly, he opened them to see the ball going towards goal. It was going in! But then the ball bounced on a clump of muddy grass. It was enough to change its direction. All he could do was to stare as the ball hit the post.

Fate had served its own justice and done what Jack could not.

If only BT invented a watch that could fast forward time, so the last few days of school would whizz by in a second and it would be the weekend. It would be the Easter break. Then he would be going away to Paris and this moment would become a distant memory. Returning to school after his holiday, everyone would have forgotten about it, hopefully.

It is amazing how many things the brain can think about in a split second. Jack's mind raced off and planned the next two weeks, while in real time, the ball had just rebounded off the woodwork. Flying off the wooden goalpost, the ball hit the back of the goalie sprawled helplessly in the mud. In slow motion, the ball ricocheted of the goalkeeper's back, sending it back towards goal. Jack stared in disbelief as the ball trickled over the goal line and into the net.

The whistle blew.

The match was over. All his teammates began hugging him and cheering. Jack had singlehandedly (by sheer fluke) won his school the Lancashire Cup!

***

School had broken up for Easter. Tomorrow was the day Jack and his friends were going on holiday. The final week of school had been an emotional rollercoaster culminating in the euphoria of Jack winning the cup final. The last two days had been brilliant.

"You've got to be kidding me!" challenged Martin. "How can you trust that backstabbing thug?"

"But who else do you know with a safe?" replied Jack.

"Yeah…I know," conceded Martin. "But him, after what he's done!"

"It's I," said Jules.

"What are you both onnabout?" asked Martin, annoyed they were not showing more interest in the important issue of why they were going to Danny's

Antiques.

"The answer's just I," Jules assured Holly. "The square root of minus one is *Imaginary*...you see? It doesn't exist. They couldn't have no solution at all, so they invented a make believe number, which is I," she explained proudly.

"But that's stupid," said Martin, half listening to their conversation. "You can't have a number that's a letter. Anyway, wait until you hear what *he's* planning on doing?" said Martin looking at Jack like he was a criminal.

"But it makes sense, don't you see?" said Jack.

"No it doesn't. You need locking up, mate. You're a loon!" replied Martin, pointing to his head and twirling his finger around.

"What're they arguing about?" Jules asked Holly.

"Haven't the faintest idea," he shrugged, equally as confused.

"I'll tell you what it's all about," said Martin, as Jack began to quicken the pace, distancing himself from the discussion. "He's taking all the stuff to Danny's."

"What stuff?" asked Holly.

"Who's Danny?" asked Jules.

"You know, he's the guy from the antiques shop."

"What does he want to bother with him for? Especially after what he did," said Jules, frowning.

"Because," Martin said labouring the point, "Mr. I-know-what-I'm-doing over there, thinks Danny can help."

27

"I can hear you, you know," said Jack, raising his voice over the noise of a car blasting its horn at some kids running across the road.

"Look! You're not making any sense at all..." said Holly, before turning his attention to Jack. "Jack...wait up! Where're you going?"

"I'm going to Danny's Antiques to take him the stuff to look after while we're away," said Jack for what felt like the fiftieth time. It was hard to believe when it came to figuring things out, Holly and Jules were normally razor sharp.

"What stuff?" wondered Jules.

"Geez," Jack shook his head in despair, "you know... those bits of treasure that I kept."

"What? The coin and the key?" asked Holly.

"Yes...and the golden right-angled thingy," explained Jack, again.

"What, are you... mad?!" stood Holly speechless.

"That's exactly what I was saying," said Martin, happy someone actually agreed with him.

BT tried to explain the plan. No one was listening to a word *he* was saying. They argued all the way into town. Jack remained adamant that he was doing the right thing. He found it hard to see why the others did not understand. It made perfect sense. All the arguing dampened Jack's excitement. They were supposed to be going on holiday in the morning.

After Jack's daring escapades during the summer

break, which involved uncovering King Richard the Second's secret, a local business had offered to give Jack and his friends a free holiday. It was good advertising for the printing company. They got loads of press and media attention on the back of Jack's brush with death.

It turned out the companies' idea of a holiday for thirteen – which consisted of Jack, his mum and dad, Jules and Martin and their mum (and subsequently new boyfriend), Holly and his younger sister and BT with both their sets of parents – was a meagre £1,000. Jack pointed out that you could not even buy a decent mountain bike for that, let alone a holiday for thirteen people – but no one listened to what he thought.

In the end, not everyone was able to go, meaning the money stretched a little further. The bad news was Holly's little sister was still coming along. Jack felt an eight-year-old was too young and certain to cramp their style. The good news was his grandad would now be coming with them. This seemed only fair. After all, if it had not been for Jack's grandad, there likely would not have been a treasure hunt in the first place.

Jack now realised he was standing outside the wrong shop. *Hilary's Health Food Emporium* was possibly the most boring shop in town. He never understood the appeal. His mum once explained that some people had special dietary conditions, and as a consequence, had to watch what they ate. Well none of that rubbish bothered Jack. He could eat anything.

Arriving at the antiques shop Jack stared through the window. Nothing looked to have changed much since he had been there eight months ago. The letter 'A' for Antiques was still missing from the sign on the door.

Martin seemed determined to have his way and in the entranceway to the shop, a mini-tussle broke out for the possession of Jack's rucksack. Before anyone could lay claim to the prized assets, the door burst open under their weight, sending them tumbling into the shop. Jack still managed to hear the brass bell jingle even though he had Martin, Jules, and Holly all squashed on top of him.

Jack somehow squirmed his way out from under the pileup and onto his feet. He was just dusting himself off and looking at the writhing mass on the floor when Danny appeared.

"What's going on?" he bellowed. "This shop isn't for... oh, erm, it's you!" Danny stumbled.

"Yes, it is, and we need a favour," explained Jack boldly, marching towards the counter.

"I'm sorry," said Danny. "I'm closed. So if you'll excuse me."

Quick as a flash, Jack cornered the man ten times his size. "Don't you dare," he berated the shopkeeper. "We know what you did and we now need you to do something for us."

"I don't know what you're talking about!" replied Danny. His t-shirt rode half way up his large belly, making it look five sizes too small.

"We can always call in at the cop-shop on our way home and tell them what we know," said BT, cutting off the large man's retreat.

"Okay, okay. Danny was just having his fun with you all, you know. Good old Danny, you see..."

Placing his rucksack on the counter, Jack's hand moved towards the zip when Martin grabbed his wrist. "Don't do it Jack. You can't trust him."

Pushing Martin's hand away, Jack proceeded to unzip his school backpack. Instead of school work or a change of sports clothes spilling out, his bag contained the ancient antiquities he had found. One by one, he pulled the key, the coin and the triangle out of his bag and placed them carefully down on the counter.

For a moment, nobody spoke. Eventually, Jack made his demands.

"Mr. Pullen, I need you to look after these for a short while. We're going away, and unfortunately, you're the only person in the world I know who has a safe. We're going on holiday and I can't leave them in my house."

For a second, Danny did not or could not speak. "Erm...yes. Alright then. Is that it? I mean it shouldn't be a problem," he finally stammered.

"Yep...I'm sure. Now you'd better not try anything funny, if you know what I mean," Jack winked at BT. "We'll be back in just over a week's time and... they'd better be safe!"

"And I've got all this sorted," said BT, tapping a badge

shaped like a gruesome looking fly, fastened to his jacket. Everyone looked at BT as though he was half mad.

"No, no, no...you take as long as you want. Rest assured." Danny threw a phony looking smile. "You can trust good old honest Dan."

"You can trust good, old, honest Dan," mimicked Martin once outside the shop, safely out of earshot "That guy's a crook and we should have let the police deal with him. That's the last we'll see of him or your treasured valuables!"

"But that's exactly why we can trust him. He knows we have this over him. If he tries it on, he knows we can just grass him up. So that's exactly why he won't! And besides, we've got insurance..." Jack immediately pointed to BT.

Holly was convinced Jack was losing his marbles. "I'm sure you got serious brain damage when The Stoneman gave you that dead leg!"

"What exactly do you mean by, 'insurance policy?'" interrupted Jules.

"See this fly fastened here?" said BT proudly tapping the odd looking badge.

"Yeah," they all echoed as one.

"It's a prototype camera that I, er...sort of...well, borrowed from my dad," explained BT. "This badge is a spy-fly that sees and hears everything and, it's connected to my mobile. I call it the sneaker-phone."

Martin, Holly, and Jules stood astonished with their

mouths open.

"It's connected to his mobile and it records everything. Like I said...*insurance!*" echoed Jack smugly.

"That's well good! Why didn't you tell us?" said Martin excitedly. His stance on the whole situation had shifted quicker than the wind changing direction.

"I tried to," said BT, "but none of you would shut up. Just because I'm the smallest and youngest, doesn't mean that you've gotta ignore everything I say!" said BT, puffing out his chest and making himself as tall as possible. "I've modified it to take video footage and store it on my mobile phone. So we've got everything covered!"

The Drawbridge

33

Chapter Four

Tossing and turning all night, Jack hardly slept a wink. The last few days seemed to have lasted a whole month. His alarm buzzed loudly. Although tired from a restless night's sleep, Jack awoke bright eyed and bushy tailed. Hurray! He was finally going on holiday.

He leaped from his bed with the athletic agility of a gazelle. His feet glided with supreme ease across the bedroom floor. Nothing could ruin his holiday. He knew it was going to be perfect. A trip to Disneyland Paris with his mates – and the best bit about it, everything was free!

He was already packed. He had never been so organised in his life. Hurriedly, he put on his new blue and white striped top and jeans.

His dad had gone out early to pick up the hire car – a bit of common sense, at last. It also meant an extra long shower without the fear of his dad banging on the bathroom door, shouting for him to get out and stop wasting all the hot water.

Desperate not to miss anything, Jack wolfed down his coco pops in record time. A horn beeped outside. His dad was back with their holiday transportation. *What could it be?* He wondered. He raced to the window and threw back the curtains. *A BMW? A Mercedes? Perhaps a...* "A Minibus!!!" he yelled in shock. Outside their house sat a tired looking minibus. It was bright yellow with white painted plastic wheel trims. "Dad's gone and got us a minibus...?" complained Jack, immediately turning to his mum for clarification knowing there must be a huge mistake.

"That's right, dear," his mother replied calmly. She wore a yellow summer dress splashed with large white flowers. His mum and the minibus looked exactly the same, Jack noted – right down to the white plastic trims. They were a perfect match. Jack groaned.

"What's he gone and hired that thing for?" complained Jack, confronting his mum over the gigantic mistake.

"So we can all fit in it, darling," said his mother with an amazing calm considering the gravity of the situation. If anyone from his school were to see him, Jack would literally die of embarrassment. The last thing he needed was to give The Stoneman yet another excuse to pick on him.

"Well," he said still annoyed, crossing his arms stubbornly. "I'm not setting a single foot inside that contraption!" Jack huffed loudly, upholding his dignity.

It did not make a blind bit of difference. Half an hour later Jack begrudgingly boarded the yellow submarine.

Altogether, there were nine going on holiday. His mum, dad, his grandad, and all Jack's best friends were going. Unfortunately, Holly's eight-year-old sister, Emma was coming along, too. Emma swung her bag, accidentally hitting him on the side of his head. Jack wished the eight-year-old girl would accidentally-on-purpose get left behind.

"Hands off if you don't mind Roger! I haven't travelled all the way around the world for nothing," said Grandad, pushing aside Roger's attempts of assistance as he clambered aboard. "I'm quite capable of managing myself, you know."

All the mums and dads put on a convincing show of sorrow as they waved their kids off. Jack figured they were inwardly celebrating freedom from their children and knew his mum and dad would jump at the chance of joining them if the minibus could drive on automatic pilot. Grandad could drive. However, after what happened with the Towneley Hall episode, he knew his mum would never allow his grandad behind the wheel, ever again.

Mr. and Mrs. Baker stood at the edge of their garden gate, both dressed in their usual kooky looking outfits. BT's dad wore a pair of white coveralls with matching, extra-long, rubber gloves and wellington boots, while Mrs. Baker wore a ghastly patterned cooking apron – normally reserved for Christmas. BT's mum towered over his eccentric inventor dad.

Mr. and Mrs. Hollingsworth were standing right up against the minibus window. Holly's mum was making strange 'cooing' noises towards her daughter, Emma, while Mr. Hollingsworth repeatedly shouting to Holly through the glass, reminding him to take care of his younger sister. Poor Holly was already deep crimson.

The biggest surprise came when Martin and Jules' mum emerged to say goodbye. She stood beside a much younger, very good looking man who also began to wave.

"Who's that?" asked Jack, turning to Martin, surprise etched over his face.

"Oh him," responded Martin with an almost nonchalant dismissal. "He's mum's new boyfriend. He's so annoying."

"How come?" asked Jack.

"Well, erm...nothing much really, but that's why he's so annoying. Everything he does is almost too nice. It's like he's an alien in disguise or sommat. Jules and me can't stand him. We're trying to hatch a plan to get rid of him."

"You talking about Reginald?" Jules leaned over, showing a sudden interest in their conversation. "Class one creep! Can you believe it? He *so* wanted to come with us on holiday. Kept going on about all the rides and how he would love it at Disneyland."

"But what's wrong with that? Some grownups like doing fun things," said Holly, glad at the reprieve from his dad's reminders and his mum's embarrassing cooing.

"They've only been together for two weeks. You would have thought he would have loved an opportunity to get some time alone with Mum – especially because me and Martin have tried everything to be around them all the time, if only just to annoy him," said Jules.

"But the weird thing about it," added Martin, as the

minibus began to splutter into life, "is he seems to enjoy us hanging around. It's so mental."

"But Mum was having none of it and put her foot down. Her exact words were 'We're looking forward to spending some quality time together.' Yuk!" Having lost interest, Jules spun around and slunk back into her seat before burying her head in a book.

"He always lets us watch what we want on TV and stuff," said Martin, as he bounced up and down testing his seat. Jack could hear the seat's underused springs groaning from the abuse.

"That does sound pretty cool. I wish I was allowed to watch whatever I wanted," said Jack, wishing his dad had been replaced by a replica robot invented by BT and programmed to obey his every command. A picture of himself lying on a Lazy Boy in front of the TV while his robot-dad brought him a tray laden with snacks and a glass of Coke flashed into his mind.

"SEATBELTS!" shouted Jack's dad, smashing the illusion.

Very soon, a great big smile spread across Jack's face. For the first ten minutes, it was the best feeling in the world – going on holiday.

Pretty soon, ten minutes had stretched to thirty ... then an hour ... then two. Why could they not be there already? The bus smelled funny too – like mucky chemical fumes you would get at a petrol station.

Every time they passed a service station, they would

stop so Grandad could visit the toilet. Then, every so often, the minibus would misfire – sounding like a gunshot. People would turn and stare at the giant mobile lemon.

Hours later Martin cried out, joyfully, "Hurray... We're here! We're here!"

Jack looked through the window in time to see a sign bearing the words: *Welcome to Dover.* The phrase, "We're here!" was a little premature. They had not even left England. And they still had to queue for the ferry. Jack thought they were never going to get out of the ugly banana-coloured bus.

Jack desperately needed the toilet. The journey had been so boring he had spent most of his time drinking fizzy pop and nibbling on bits of junk food. Now, he desperately needed the toilet. The yellow sherbet lemon spluttered to a halt. Jack looked out of the minibus as they parked in the belly of the ferry. It was surprisingly dark and gloomy.

Unable to wait any longer, Jack charged through the crowd of people heading for the steps that led to the main part of the ferry. Making sure he was first, he raced up the flight of stairs and turned to find himself on the outside gangway. Looking out over the side, he could see the sea. For a moment, he forgot about his pressing need for the bathroom. This was the first time he had ever been on a boat – apart from the paddle boat in the local park – which theoretically did not count.

A little aching feeling below told him to hurry up, or else. Jack raced off along the gangway unsure what direction he should be going.

He turned a corner, and before he could hit the brakes, *bang!*

"Ouch!" said Jack, rubbing his side as he landed on the floor with a bump.

"I am terribly sorry," said a woman in a soft voice, tinged with a foreign accent.

From the metal gangway, Jack looked up to see a tall and elegant woman, her beautiful face peering out from under a black fur-lined hat. Wearing a matching full-length fur coat, the woman towered above him. If Jules had been there, Jack was certain she would have gone on about cruelty to animals and how many poor bunny rabbits would have been chopped up just to make one coat.

A black satin-gloved hand reached out to Jack offering to help him to his feet. He was fine! She took hold of his hand anyway. The woman had just helped him up when the ferry, leaving its mooring, jerked into life. They were off. He was officially at sea for the first time in his life.

The force of the judder caused Jack and the strange woman, who still had hold of his hand, to collide. Something fell from underneath her fur coat and clattered onto the deck, right by Jack's feet.

An ornate wooden box lay there. Jack bent down to pick it up. As he reached out to grab the box, he noticed an emblem inlaid on the lid. The symbols tugged at his memory and made him hesitate. He was sure he had seen the symbols somewhere before.

Before he could grasp the box, he felt himself tumbling over. This time, it was no accident.

"Stupid boy," sniped the woman as she picked up her possession. "Watch where you're walking next time!"

Bamboozled by what had just taken place, Jack stayed sat on the floor, attempting to understand what had just happened. As he got to his feet, a small white object lying on the floor caught his eye. Seconds later, he was holding a soft lace handkerchief. In one of the corners, the letters E.C. were embroidered in royal blue surrounded by a golden circle. He figured that E.C. was probably the woman's initials and he put the dainty handkerchief into his pocket in case he saw her again. He still needed to find the toilet.

***

It took Jack nearly an hour of aimless wandering before he finally found his friends and family. There were literally hundreds of corridors and flights of stairs in almost every direction. They were settling down into one of the cabins. It was a tiny room and definitely not designed for three adults and six kids. The idea was they had somewhere to relax – if one could call being squashed tighter than a hamster in a matchbox, relaxing.

Jack stood in a corner out of the way of the mayhem. Over and over, he kept reliving the accidental collision.

He struggled to understand what he might have done to upset the woman. He knew he was missing a vital clue.

After spending ten minutes packed like human sardines, his mum and dad left the room. Much to Jack's relief, Grandad took Emma with him to the on-board cinema. For some reason, she kept hovering around him wherever he went. She devised silly excuses to get Jack's attention – like offering to show him her latest school project. And he thought Holly was bad! It was so obvious they were related. The only difference being Emma was more interested in geography than history. And she was supposed to be shy.

Soon, the five friends were laughing and joking, planning what rides they wanted to go on. Martin started teasing BT about his height and how the only rides he would be allowed on would be the baby rides. Their laughter at the hilarious image of BT scrunched up inside a child's car on a merry-go-round was interrupted by a knock on the cabin door.

Jack's first thought was his mum must have forgotten to take a key. He sprang to open the door. A young boy dressed in a smart, white uniform took Jack by surprise.

"Can you come to the family lounge, please?" he asked politely.

"What for?" Jack asked the spotty-faced teenager.

"I don't know," he said. "Captain's orders! Everyone has to go there… now!"

"Captain's orders," laughed Martin in a sarcastic voice

as they made their way into the lounge. "Ferries don't have captains," he said. "Only real ships have captains."

"This is an outrage," a smartly-dressed man with silver hair, bushy moustache and large sideburns turned and complained to Jack, as though he had known him all his life. "I have been travelling for years and this is the first time this has ever happened. I have an extremely important business meeting to prepare for and I have no time to be wasting on some fool's errand." The man wagged his finger accusingly at one of the crew members who happened to pass by. "This is simply preposterous!" he spluttered, his bushy moustache flapping as he spoke. Sheepishly the crewman hurried on his way, ignoring the man.

As more people continued cramming into the already overflowing lounge area, the temperature became uncomfortable. As always, Jack's dad succeeded in embarrassing him in front of the whole room by shouting, "Jacky! We're over here!" half way across the lounge. It was impossible to hear his friends speak over the excited chatter in the room.

"Can I have your attention, please?" said a man who was barely audible above the buzz in the room.

"CAN I HAVE..." the man's voice boomed. Someone had switched the microphone on twenty settings too high. A sharp, piercing noise lanced through Jack's ears, splitting his head in two. "I must profusely apologise for that," flustered the man.

Jack's ears were still ringing from the incompetent use of the ferry's P.A. equipment when the man spoke again at a more acceptable level. Jack wanted to blame the newly recruited cabin boy who had knocked on their door earlier. He pictured the spotty-faced teenager putting the wires into the wrong connections.

"I regret to inform you that we have had an imprudent misappropriation of an incalculable proportion," the announcement came.

"A mis-calcul-what?" asked Jack, turning around and looking at his friends for an explanation.

"Did you understand any of that?" asked BT with an equally blank expression.

"I think there's been a murder," gasped Martin.

"What he's actually saying…" shouted Jules just as silence settled over the room. Jules' cheeks suddenly flushing with embarrassment as she tamely finished her sentence, "something valuable has been stolen!"

Chapter Five

"Good afternoon, ladies and gentleman." Jack glanced up to see a very official looking man wearing a long grey overcoat. If the films Jack watched were anything to go by, then he figured the man must be connected to the police.

"My name is Roger Gante and I work for Interpol. I must apologise for the untimely inconvenience. My intentions are to carry out an expeditious recovery of the misappropriated items with as ephemeral a detainment as possible."

An excited gabble washed across the lounge. Jack could not believe how unfair this all was. What if the ferry was ordered to return to England? What if they were stuck out at sea for days? Either way could drastically affect his holiday.

"Did he just say Interpol? That's so cool. It's like something out of one of my spy books," piped BT.

"This is all very unusual, don't you think?" Jules asked in her typical, calm manner. Jack simply agreed without understanding what Jules was referring to. He hadn't understood a single word the man from Interpol had said.

They were all forced to wait in the ferry's family lounge for the next two hours. They were all given a free drink of pop, which Holly thought was fantastic.

To break the boredom, Martin suggested playing the game, 'Guess the Master Criminal.' Holly thought the stuffy businessman who had tried talking to them earlier would make a good suspect. BT decided the short man with a bright red face and bushy beard standing a couple of feet away could easily be a clever disguise for a mass murderer. Jack's guess was the woman he had bumped into earlier. None of his friends believed she existed and he ended up choosing the spotty faced crew boy, much to Martin and BT's derision.

Two hours finally passed. The boredom now over, they could go back to enjoying their trip. Jack was relieved. The unpleasantness of the ferry turning around and going straight back home without ever seeing France had crossed his mind on several occasions.

Later that evening, after the excitement or boredom of the day – depending on how one viewed it – they found somewhere private to hang out. It felt good to be away from prying eyes. The thought of their every move being watched by their parents or other adults was no fun.

"What do you reckon about this afternoon, then?" said Jack, hoping a conversation about stolen valuables would take his mind away from the boat's back and forth motion. Although his friends had said otherwise, he could feel his face turning a shade of seasick green. Unfortunately, there was no mirror on hand to confirm his worst thoughts.

"I thought the free pop was well good," laughed

Martin as he let out a timely belch.

"If only they would have given us free snacks as well," bemoaned Holly. The talk of food reminded him about the chocolate-coated fruit bar he still had in his pocket. He ripped the wrapper off in super quick time. In one single bite, half the bar was gone.

"Why would someone working for Interpol even be on this ferry to Calais in the first place, unless... they were already tracking some sort of international criminal?" Jules pointed out.

"Cool!" exclaimed Martin. "A master criminal on board this ferry! We could have seen him already without even realising it."

"What do you mean... *him*?" challenged Jules. "Why do you automatically assume that a master criminal could only be a man? It could quite easily be a woman."

For a split second, the four boys burst out laughing. Although Jack figured, if there was a woman with the same brain power of Jules, she could easily be a top criminal if she put her mind to it.

"Does anyone want a chuddy?" asked Jack as he finished laughing, pulling out the remnants of a squashed packet from his pocket. "Oh! I've only got two pieces left."

"What's that?" asked Jules looking confused.

"It's what we call chewing gum," explained Jack in a fake aristocratic voice.

"No! Not that, you moron! I know what chewing gum is! That!" Jules bent down and picked up something white and dainty with a lace trim around the edges.

"Uh, I found it this morning when we first got here. Some posh woman dropped it," Jack explained.

"What, it was just lying around?"

"No silly. I tried telling you about that snotty woman I bumped into earlier," explained Jack.

"You didn't say that," said Jules, tersely.

"What snotty woman?" asked Holly.

"I did!" Jack protested. "It belonged to that posh looking woman. I bumped into her when I was on the way to the toilet. She was nice to start with, but suddenly turned funny. I told you earlier I thought she was the mastermind that Interpol's chasing, but you wouldn't believe me."

"What makes you think *she* could be the master criminal?" asked BT.

"We were practically the first car–" Holly started to say.

"Bus," corrected Martin. "It's a bus, not a car."

"Whatever! As I was saying, we were the first *bus*," exclaimed Holly throwing Martin a scornful look. "How could another passenger already be on board? You ran off to find the toilet before anyone else could have boarded the ferry. So..." Holly paused for dramatic effect, "how could she already be on the ferry?"

"Well, she could just be one of the workers," BT pointed out.

"That wouldn't fit. Her clothes were too expensive

looking to be just a worker," observed Jack, trying to retrace the events in his mind.

"What if she had fallen asleep and missed her stop. Then, when you bumped into her she was trying to get off?" suggested Martin. For once, it appeared Martin had made a valid point.

Jack felt something was fishy. Not the fact they were in the middle of the English Channel fishy – the other kind of fishy.

"Look at this," interrupted Jules, waving the posh handkerchief in the air.

"It's a snot rag for grownups," said Martin.

"Yeah," Jules rolled her eyes, "but look at the insignia."

"So it's a *posh* snot rag then?" Martin giggled.

"The letters, E.C. in this fancy motif," she pointed out. "I've seen them before. I'm almost positive they belong to Elizabeth Coldaire."

"And who's she when she's at home?" asked BT.

"Who's she? Don't you know anything?" scoffed Jules. "She's only a very famous French actress!"

"That's cool. I wish I had a name like Dare... Martin 'Dare' Brown. It's got a certain ring to it, don't ya think?" said Martin as he crouched down, pretending his hands were a gun.

"Shurrup weasel head! And how do you know who she is, Jules?" asked Holly, before giving Martin a gentle shove. Martin pushed back.

"Will you two pack it in!" ordered Jules. "And for

your information, I know this because she's in all the latest magazines. Maybe it's time to change your reading habits?"

"I'm not reading any sissy mags," said Holly, defending his obvious lack of knowledge on the subject.

"But if she's as famous as you say she is, then why would she be on *this* ferry? Wouldn't she be on some flash jet?" questioned Jack.

"Well, that's the interesting part. She's always using every available opportunity to hog the limelight. If she'd been to England, the press would have been all over the story. There would be pictures of her everywhere, except..." Jules paused with excitement, "there's been nothing. It's almost like she doesn't want anyone to know she's been to England, or... on this ship!"

"I, for one, agree with Jules," BT joined in. "Maybe she was carrying something important and she didn't want anyone to know–"

"That's right!" interrupted Jack excitedly. Inside his head a million light bulbs switched on simultaneously. "And you're never going to believe what she had with her! I knew something didn't add up! I'd forgotten all about it. But..."

"What?" the other four said all at once, turning and looking at him in eager anticipation.

"I think I know what's been stolen!" announced Jack.

Chapter Six

"What do you mean, you know what was st-st-stolen–"
The clang of a metal door slamming shut interrupting
Martin.

"What are you doing in here?" a tall man in uniform
asked. "This is restricted for staff only," the crewman
warned. "Now beat it!"

They did not need a second invitation. Jack sprinted
through the door, the others mere steps behind him.
They all ran along a couple of corridors, then up a flight
of steps. Pushing open another door that led to the upper
deck, Jack charged through before coming to an abrupt
halt. A wave crashed over the side of the boat. Before he
could retreat backwards, water sprayed him from head to
toe. A ripple of laughter erupted behind him.

"What?" he moaned. Not for the first time that week,
he now looked like a drowned clown – which is worse
than a drowned rat.

They moved to a safer spot at the front of the boat, away
from the clutches of the mocking sea and sat down on
sun bleached orange plastic chairs. Jack understood why
none of the other passengers were out on deck. Although
the sky was blue, a bitter cold wind tore right across the
front of the ferry. The vessel rocked as menacing waves
licked at its sides.

The plastic chairs were not only wet, but also

extremely uncomfortable, realised Jack sitting down. The boat crashed through another wave on the choppy sea. As far as the eye could see – a gazillion, gazillion gallons of water. Jack thought that was a lot of water! *Where did it all come from and why did it not drain away?* He wondered. Whenever he had been to the beach and built a sandcastle and poured water into his sand moat, it soaked straight through. *So why did the sea not soak through the sand bed, which was lining the bottom of the oceans?* Jack remembered hearing on the news once that the sea was getting higher and one day lots of places like London and New York would simply vanish underwater. None of it made any sense.

"So come on then, don't keep us waiting in suspense…" Martin nudged Jack from his watery ponderings.

"Oh right! Yeah," said Jack jolting back to reality. "So, this is what happened: When the boat set off, it juddered and she fell into me, dropping a box she had been clutching under her coat."

"So you're saying someone stole *her* box?" said Martin sarcastically.

"Yeah," responded Jack, "but the wooden box looked just like the one we found in the tunnel back in Towneley Hall."

For a minute, no one spoke. Only the sound of the wind whistling around the upper deck punctuated the silence. Not a single seagull could be heard squawking.

"What? The same one?" said Jules, realising from

everyone's puzzled looks that she had phrased her question badly. She rephrased it. "I mean… did it look like the one we found with the same markings on it?" she asked, careful to speak clearly.

"No," protested Jack. "Not the same one! This one looked different, but it was the same, if you know what I mean." The others stared blankly at Jack. "I'm just saying it was the same kind of old…but it had a gold image on the lid that I didn't recognise. But you're not going to believe this, I'm sure it half looked like the symbol of the Four Corners."

"No way!" whistled BT.

"Well, why didn't you tell us earlier?" demanded Holly, momentarily standing up while he tried to wipe the water off his chair with his sleeve.

"Because, I kinda didn't have chance," responded Jack. "There were always my mum and dad and even Emma hovering around. She's behind me almost everywhere I turn," he insisted before jumping up and bouncing on his toes to bring back his circulation. The sea wind was whistling right through him. There was no sign of spring on the channel. Jack licked his lips only for the bitter taste of sea salt to catch his senses unaware.

"What… are you mad?" shouted Holly. "After everything we went through in the summer…you see an image of the Four Corners and you don't even bother to tell us!"

"I know," admitted Jack. "But, somehow, it didn't look

the same and it was all confusing," he finished lamely.

"Well, either it was or it wasn't. Make your mind up," said Martin, leaping out of his seat just as an extraordinarily large wave crashed over the side. There was no escaping the spray from the sea.

"I'm not sure. She pushed me over and grabbed it before I could have a proper look," protested Jack. "But it definitely was the symbol with the cross and everything. It just sort of looked...a bit odd, is all I'm saying."

"Are you sure Jack?" said Jules taking him more seriously than the rest of his friends.

"Course I am!" exclaimed Jack, indignantly.

"Well, I don't get it," Holly went on. "It can't be the same, but then not. I mean did it have the three lions on it, as well?"

"No, I don't think so," said Jack, trying to conjure up an image of what he had seen.

"Well, there you are then…" said Holly, "case closed!" And bowed in front of the others like a court jester.

"It all seems very peculiar to me," said Jules, hesitantly. "But I believe you Jack. I'm, in."

"Yeah, me too," agreed BT.

"And me," said Martin, busy twirling around like an out of control helicopter.

"But-t, you heard what he said...right? It sounds like…" huffed Holly, looking to his friends for support. After pausing briefly, "well alright then," Holly relented, before shaking his finger at Jack. "But you'd better be right."

"So we're all agreed then. We need to find that box," orchestrated Jules while the boys were busy giving each other high fives.

Jack smiled. He was leading them on a treasure hunt, again!

The Outer Courtyard

Chapter Seven

The journey from Dover to Calais was taking forever. By Jack's reckoning, they had already been at sea for more than five hours.

Stuck at sea for days or even weeks would be a disaster. Martin suggested their boat had been hijacked by terrorists. Holly, as usual, wanted to know what would happen about food supplies. They could not simply send someone out for pizzas. Even if they flew food in by helicopter, how many pizzas would you need for a thousand people? And what toppings would everyone want? They never explain how they resolve that in the movies, BT pointed out.

Bored with playing cards with his friends, Jack decided to set off to explore the ferry. He was hoping to spot the famous film star he had bumped into earlier.

At every turn, there seemed to be another corridor. Jack had been daydreaming and found himself away from the hustle and bustle of the ferry. Sometimes at school, he would imagine he was the world's greatest footballer. Today, however, he was a top government undercover agent on the trail of the world's most dangerous criminal mastermind.

He had been on their trail for six months. No one had ever lasted that long once Jack Hunter was on the case. He knew it was only a matter of time until he apprehended the culprit and, once again, gained worldwide recognition for his clever arrest.

Ahead, he heard a door creak loudly. He looked up to see it swing outwards, revealing the sign; *Platinum Suite – Members Only. This would be the perfect hideout for a rich and famous film actress,* thought Jack. The only problem, he was not a member. Yet he was no ordinary boy – he was Agent Hunter, super sleuth!

A young couple, arms linked, stepped out through the door, laughing. Jack froze. Thankfully, they were too busy to notice him. They strolled off in the opposite direction. If he sprinted the short distance, perhaps Jack could reach the door before it swung shut.

Jack ran quietly on the balls of his feet imagining himself in an anti-gravitational chamber. He was going to be the first youth-spy to be sent into outer space. The door had almost shut but his training was not to be in vain. He wrapped his fingers over the lip of the solid metal door just in time. Luckily, the door was fitted with a slow closing mechanism. As he silently slipped through the open door, the couple were already disappearing around the corner and out of sight.

Crouching down, Jack glanced left, then right. The coast was clear for Agent Hunter. Not only did the room appear deserted, but it was unlike anywhere else on the boat. The seats were covered in a plush velvet fabric – the same colour as blackcurrants. Plasma TV's were generously dotted along the walls. In an unlit corner a cocktail bar stood. There was even a mirrored ceiling.

The door clicked shut behind him, the noise echoing through the empty suite. A rumble emitted from his stomach cutting through the silence. His body reminded him he had not eaten for hours. Suddenly, he remembered who he was. He was no secret agent or super sleuth. He was just an ordinary twelve-year-old boy, called Jack.

Reality seized hold of him. He was not supposed to be there. Spinning around Jack headed for the exit. That is when he saw the handle turning. Panic seized him. He was trapped. There was only one door in, one door out. He looked around the room for somewhere to hide. A bright red, flashing, luminous sign lit up inside his head – the cocktail bar!

Jack landed behind the counter just as he heard the door snap shut. His optimistic theory that someone had opened the wrong door was cruelly smashed. Someone began to speak.

"You sure we are safe in here?" Jack heard a man say with a strong Eastern European accent.

"I keep telling you, Vladimir, stop worrying," his partner replied in an American accent.

"I cannot get it to open, Mikhail," said Vladimir. "The lock is jammed."

"Look, just get on with it. You know what'll happen if we fail," said the American. "And Vladimir..."

"What Mikhail?"

"Stop calling me Mikhail. I'm now Michael,

remember?!"

"Mikhail...Michael, it is all very much the same to me."

"I didn't go through all that hard work and learn this accent for nothing. Remember that! One slip and you'll blow my cover."

Instantly, Jack realised these two men were not the clientele normally associated with the Platinum Suite. They sounded more like gangsters.

Not again!

He must be the unluckiest boy alive. At the rate Jack was going, he would soon know half the underworld population – and he was only twelve!

"What's the knife for?"

Jack gulped. That settled it. They were definitely criminals.

"So I open it," replied Vladimir. "It is stuck," he noted.

"Well hurry up then," urged Michael. "We don't have much time."

Jack's stomach began rumbling, again. Of all the times it had to remind him he was hungry, was now!

"What was that noise?" asked Vladimir.

"It's nothing, probably just your imagination running wild. Get a move on will you, before somebody comes," replied Michael.

"There, I have gotten it open," said Vladimir. "Keep watch on the door, *Michael*."

So one was definitely Russian and the second man

used to be Russian, but now sounds American. He was once Mikhail but is now Michael, Jack duly noted. It was more than a little confusing.

Jack listened hard. *What were they up to? What were they looking for?* He wondered.

"It's not here!" said Vladimir, sounding distraught. "What should we do?"

"I don't know. Are you sure? It's got to be. George said it would be in the box," explained Michael.

"I only good looking one! You supposed to be the intelligence," quipped Vladimir. *So they are the thieves!* Jack figured. Of all the rotten luck in the world, he happened to be hiding in the same room with the very two people wanted by Interpol.

Jack started to get a stiff neck and stretched it skywards. His heart literally missed a beat at what he saw: The two bad guys, only upside down. Jack had forgotten all about the mirrored ceiling. It only meant one thing: If he could see them, they would be able to see him!

"We could take the jewels, no? They will be worth very expensive."

"No Vladimir. He said take nothing other than the key. Now be quiet while I think. Shush... What was that?"

Squashed up awkwardly behind the cocktail bar, Jack was beginning to get pins and needles sensations. Stretching out his leg, he accidentally tapped an empty bottle lying close by. He felt a funny sensation whoosh through the pit of his stomach.

"Look," said Vladimir.

Jack buried his head in his knees, scrunched his eyes tight, and held his breath. He knew it would not help, but for some reason it made him feel a little safer. For that millisecond, if he could wish for any super power in the whole world, it would definitely be invisibility.

"There's a bar! Free vodka, my friend."

The sound of footsteps treading across the deep pile carpet to where he hid sent a shiver along Jack's spine. He became sick with dread.

They were getting closer.

"Not now! We have to find the key. The boss said it would definitely be in the box. I reckon someone has beaten us to it. We had better fix this. Otherwise, there'll be trouble…" said Michael, sounding anxious.

The footsteps stopped at the other side of the bar. A metre-wide wooden frame was all that separated Jack from a Russian mobster, with a knife!

"Michael, just one drink…Yes?" Vladimir pleaded.

"Later…" said Michael firmly.

Jack could not breathe. His body ached from clenching his muscles so tightly. A slight relief washed over him as the man walked further away. The sound of footsteps stopped. It was followed by an eerie silence.

With the speed of a slug, Jack opened his eyes and blinked at the ceiling. The men were nowhere to be seen. It appeared they had left the room. He uncurled his body. Every muscle throbbed. It could almost have been a dream.

A chrome-top bin stood by a pillar in the middle of the room. This particular waste bin had something poking out of its top. Made from dark wood and looking antique, a moment of surprise hit him. Elizabeth Coldaire's stolen box. It had to be.

Jack rushed over, quickly rescuing the box from its unworthy resting place. Placing it gently on one of the velvet seats, he noticed the outer casing was splintered where Vladimir had abruptly forced it open with his knife.

After all Jack had been through, the last thing he wanted to be doing was getting deeper involved. However, curiosity quickly took over his sense of fear.

Hesitantly, Jack flipped the splintered lid open.

Chapter Eight

What he saw took his breath away. Gold necklaces, bracelets encrusted with jewels, and rings with diamonds the size of aniseed balls threatened to spill out of the compartments in the wooden box. Most people could only dream of holding so much wealth in their hands. But, Jack wasn't *most* people.

Last summer, Jack had found a king's ransom in gold coins and precious artefacts. The haul was so large that, even now, they were still checking it off, cleaning and cross referencing it. One man had told him, "In years to come kids up and down the country will be reading about you, Jack Hunter, in their history books."

Jack just shrugged his shoulders. It would be much cooler if they were reading about him because he scored the winning goal in the world cup final he thought.

Staring blankly at the jewellery box, Jack found it difficult to comprehend why the crooks were not interested in stealing the jewels. That's what thieves do! So what was different? It did not make any sense. He ran through the events in his mind one more time.

Closing the box Jack looked at the symbol engraved on the outside of the lid. It definitely looked like the mark of the Four Corners. Even the four small hands were placed around it. Yet there was something not quite right. Jack remembered pressing the symbol on the fire surround in Towneley Hall like a button. This cross looked a lot less like a button and a lot more like an expensive decoration. The intricately carved golden symbol into the highly polished surface could easily be mistaken as being seven months old, not seven hundred years.

Curiosity told him to try pushing it. He held his breath. Nothing happened. As he pulled his finger away, he was sure something looked different. The whole image had moved ever so slightly.

With shaking fingers, Jack touched the symbol again. Only this time, instead pushing down on the symbol like a button, he tried sliding it around like a dial. He was right! It began to move. Picturing the image of the Four Corners, he turned the centre circle into position.

Just as the symbol fell into the right place, there was a faint click. A secret silk-lined drawer shot open. Nestled in the middle minding its own business, was a key. It wasn't just any household key, but ancient, just like the one he had found back in England.

The last time Jack poked his nose innocently into where it did not belong, he nearly got himself and his friends killed. In order to avoid an inevitable fatal disaster, the obvious course of action would be to take the key and the box to the Inspector from Interpol. With a mind of its own, Jack's hand dropped like a claw crane from an amusement arcade. He was an unwilling spectator while his brain manoeuvred the control stick and skilfully picked up the prized object.

When he felt the key inside his pocket, he closed the secret compartment. The tray clicked shut. The symbol within the circle then moved back into its original position, eliminating the evidence. Jack knew he had to get out of the Platinum Suite, and fast. If those guys changed their minds, he would be trapped.

Keeping hold of the box, Jack shot through the door faster than a speeding bullet. He ran along the corridor and down another level before his brain paused for directions. He needed to be around people. That way he would be safe, but where?

The family lounge. That is where he last saw the man from Interpol. There would be plenty of people around, for sure. But, he could not remember how to get there. He was lost.

Whether by sheer fluke, or the fact his brain had subconsciously mapped out every room he had visited, Jack managed to find the lounge. It was nearly half past seven in the evening, yet the place was still full of people.

Jack spotted a man sporting a decorative hat, looking suspiciously like the ship's captain.

"Excuse me, sir," said Jack tugging on the man's jacket from behind. As the man turned round, Jack held out the box. "I think I found it," he panted.

The captain looked at him and then at the box and then back at Jack. "Would you like to come with me?" he said, turning around and walking away. For one split-second Jack hesitated before hurrying after the captain through a door marked, *Private*. Jack felt nervous, but special, as he scuttled through the door.

"Hello, Roger," said the ship's captain as he entered the room. "I have someone I think you should meet." With that, he turned and left Jack standing there.

The door slammed shut. Jack felt alone. He was in a room similar in size to the headmaster's office at school. The man from Interpol sat behind a desk with his back to him. For a moment, Jack felt as though he were back in Mr. Rumble's office, ready for another lecture.

He knew the routine by heart. First, the headmaster would pretend there was no one there. Next, he'd spin around on his chair and act surprised. Then, which was the best bit, old Crumble would ask what he could do for Jack – almost as if he did not have a clue why Jack was there.

The vision of Crumble's office disappeared as soon as Jack heard the sound of the chair creaking. He watched with bated breath as the man spun round. "Well," he said with a surprised look. "What can I do for you, young man?" He almost looked unimpressed by Jack's presence. Jack inwardly smiled. Grownups were *so* predictable.

"I-I th-think," stammered Jack, his mouth dry and sticky. "I think I've found the stolen thing that was stolen."

The stolen thing that was stolen! Jack replayed the phrase in his head. He could have kicked himself for sounding so dumb. Quickly he held out the box.

"Put it on the desk. Thank you." There was a long silence. "May I ask, where did you locate the box?"

"Oh! It was in the Platinum Suite, stuffed in a bin," replied Jack, enthusiastically.

"And what, might I ask, were you doing in the Platinum Suite? I'm led to believe that is a *members only* area of the ship."

Rumbled!

An alarm bell rang loudly inside Jack's head.

"I was looking for my dad," said Jack, patting himself on the back, not only for the swiftness, but also the brilliance of his reply. Unfortunately, from the emotionless expression on the Inspector's face, Jack could tell he was not impressed. Then the Interpol man leaned back on his chair. In an attempt to salvage the situation, Jack blurted out, "And then I was behind the bar because I tripped when two men came in."

The man then leaned forward, screwing up his face before springing back to Mr. Expressionless. "Did you by happenchance catch a glimpse of these two men?"

"Uh, no... well I mean uh, yea. Well sort of. I saw them upside down," spluttered Jack.

"Upside down?" asked the man from Interpol.

"Yes... Well I was hiding, right?" Jack hurried to explain. "And they were standing in the mirror. But I was pretty scared and I didn't really look properly..." finished Jack in a rush.

"You're not making much sense," the man complained. "At least could you tell me in *actual English*, if that's not too much trouble...?" Jack quickly nodded. "...did they have any distinguishing marks or characteristics?" he asked, picking up a pencil ready to write Jack's comments down in his notepad.

"I don't really know," admitted Jack, sheepishly. "It was difficult to tell because they were standing on their heads. Uh, well no!" he added. "They weren't literally... What I mean is... They were upside down and one was called Vladimir and his friend was called Mikhail, but he sounded American and not foreign like you would think with a name like that, the American, not the Russian, who then changed his name to Michael, which made it even more confusing..." said Jack as fast as he could, finally gasping for air. "Oh, and one of them didn't have much hair on top."

"So, let me get this straight... I'm searching for two upside-down male Caucasians wearing fictitious name badges, one of whom has a receding hairline?" said the Interpol man snapping shut his empty notepad.

Jack prayed for the ground to swallow him up. He was both the victim and the hero. Yet he felt more like the criminal.

"They did say that their boss was called George," remembered Jack suddenly.

"Did you say, George?" At last, Jack had got the man's attention. "If this is true, these are very dangerous men.

You are a *very, lucky,* young boy!"

Jack had a feeling of déjà vu. No matter where he went, trouble followed.

"Did you hear about the Mona Lisa being misappropriated last month? That was George Martin. We've been after him for six years. He operates a notorious international criminal organisation."

Jack shook his head slowly from side to side. He could not understand half the words the man said. In a way, it reminded him of his dad. If only Jules were there, she would be able to interpret.

"We believe he did it. In fact, a few years ago, he famously stole another historic painting and cut it up into postcard size pieces."

Jack was not sure what the inspector was talking about. He did not understand why someone would steal a valuable painting and then chop it up.

"It was a stroke of genius," the man continued. "With every exit out of the city blockaded, it would have been only a matter of time before we would have located them and retrieved the painting. Only George posted it out of the country. And he would have gotten away with it. Thankfully for us, a vigilant postal worker thought one of the postcards appeared strange. Without the missing piece, the painting became worthless to them."

"Oh, right," Jack nodded.

After the Interpol man talked further about keeping away from suspicious looking characters and being given a fifty euro note as a reward for finding the box, the man said Jack could go. The stolen artefact would now be returned to its rightful owner.

"You mean Elizabeth Coldaire?" blurted Jack without thinking.

The man paused briefly. "The famous actress? What led you to draw that conclusion?"

It had been a long day and Jack was tired. All he wanted to do was go back to his cabin, find his mum and dad, and get off the boat. "It's a long story," he replied having misgivings about opening his mouth. His parents always said that when they did not want to go into an explanation. The man got up out of his seat, and stepping awkwardly around his desk, moved towards Jack. He was an odd looking man with perfectly combed hair, a newly pressed suit and shiny gold tie clip. The toes of his shoes looked like they had never seen a tin of polish. He was also in possession of one neatly placed spare tire around his waist. The inspector then pulled something out of his pocket. Jack took a step back.

To Jack's amazement, it actually worked. The man did not ask Jack how he knew that the box belonged to the famous actress. Instead, he handed Jack a very flash looking business card. "We could do with a bright chap like you," the inspector told Jack. "Maybe, one day, you might think about joining us at Interpol. Here is my personal number. If you hear or find anything, night or day, you can always ring me."

Jack placed the business card in his pocket. As he did so, his fingertips brushed a cold, hard object. The key!

"Is there anything else you wish to tell me?" asked the Inspector, his dark eyes boring into Jack's.

Jack's mouth was as dry as a bone. *Had the man noticed his reaction?* He wondered. *Should he tell him about the key?* Jack figured giving the inspector the key would mean he could relax and enjoy the rest of his holiday with his friends. No more bad guys. For some strange reason, although he was determined to keep away from trouble, Jack threw the man a blank look.

"You're a very bright boy. Make sure you keep away from mayhem next time. By the way, I didn't catch your name," the inspector noted, offhandedly.

"It's Jack...er, Hunter," mumbled Jack.

"Not *the* Jack Hunter? The very one who found the medieval treasure last summer?" asked the inspector, surprised.

Nodding, Jack felt his face go redder than a ripe tomato.

"Well, I am indeed honoured," said the Inspector.

Chapter Nine

Soon they would be arriving in Calais. It had been a *very* long journey. Jack was looking forward to getting off the boat so he could be as far away from the two Russian gangsters as possible.

"What… He said that? Honestly? Like he'd actually knew who you were?" said BT.

"Yeah, like I was famous or something," said Jack excited from his brush with Interpol.

"What a big dollop of elephant dung," replied Martin, as he stretched a piece of chewing gum out of his mouth and twirling it around his finger.

"He did, and he said I could be a secret agent when I'm older as well," retorted Jack.

Looking at Jack with scepticism, Holly, BT, Martin, and Jules all smirked. They were supposed to be his friends. Only Emma appeared to believe him.

"Well, I think it's well ace. I think you'll make a *great* secret agent, Jack," commented Emma staring up at him.

"What're you doing here?" snapped Holly at his sister. "I thought you were supposed to be going for something to eat with Jack's mum." Without waiting for a response, he manoeuvred Emma out of the cabin and locked the door behind her.

Emma began banging on the door, threatening to tell her parents about Holly's behaviour when they returned home. "Well at least *she* believed me," said Jack loudly. "It's all true. And..." he paused for effect, "...he gave me this."

He thought it was pretty poor that he had to provide evidence to his best friends to prove he was not making the whole story up.

Exhibit A: the fancy business card.

"See," he said, flashing the card, "Roger Gante, M.I."

"Is that it?" sniggered BT.

"Wow! Looks more like one of those cards you swipe through an electronic door at a secret government laboratory than an actual business card," said Holly, snatching it from Jack's grasp. "It feels like it's made from some form of composite carbon material too...very flash!"

"What does *M.I.* stand for?" asked Martin.

"I don't know. Probably as in M.I.5 or something," replied Jack.

"I bet it stands for Mega Inspector," observed BT.

"The 'I' could stand for Interpol," Holly pointed out.

"Yeah, but you're not going to have Mega Interpol are you? That wouldn't make any sense would it?" scoffed Martin, trying to snatch the card so he could take a closer look.

"And another thing," added Jack, "he was telling *me* about this super-gangster called George Martin!"

"Did you say the gangster was called *Martin?*" interrupted Holly with a smirk on his face. "Ha-ha."

"Yeah, apparently he's the boss of a top criminal organisation. And there's this one time they stole a well expensive painting worth millions and chopped it up into postcards or sommat. That is what he was saying anyway, I think," said Jack, with a frown.

"No thief is going to steal a million dollar painting and then cut it up. That'd make it worthless," disagreed Jules.

"Now that's where you're wrong. I thought that at first too," said Jack excitedly. "But then I remembered my mum. She ripped a twenty pound note in half, by accident, yeah. But then she stuck it back together right and used it at the supermarket. It was still worth twenty quid…see?!" replied Jack proudly.

Jules moved her lips, but then quickly closed her mouth. Jack had outwitted the super smart Jules for the first time. He was on fire!

The new version of the events remarkably evolved considering how Jack was scared witless at the time. With his friend's complete and undivided attention he continued describing in detail the large casket of jewels and how he was trapped by the six, really large, Russian gangsters. They carried huge, razor-sharp knives and deadly machine guns.

Even Roger Gante, M.I. had grown an extra foot taller as Jack went on to recall how he outsmarted the Interpol man. The new and embellished account of events featured Jack sitting in the chair and asking the

Inspector all the questions.

Jack was having the time of his life. Having finished his extraordinary account, he sat down. Retrieving the souvenir from his adventure from Martin (the Inspector's business card), he placed it smugly into his pocket. As he did so, his fingers brushed against something cold and hard. The key! He had forgotten all about it. How could he have been so forgetful?

Exhibit B: the second centuries-old-key that, by chance, had come into Jack's possession in a little over eight months.

The whole episode seemed too unbelievable to be true. If there was any doubt in their minds about his story, including the bad guys, this would squash them as effectively as an out-of-control steamroller rolling down a steep hill.

Standing in the centre of the cabin, Jack proudly lifted the medieval key in the air. Not only to show it off, but to keep it out of harm's way. The key was practically touching the light bulb when something intriguing caught Jack's eye.

"I think there's some numbers on the key," observed Jack as he brought it swiftly down for closer inspection.

The key was very ornate. A stunning green crystal sat in the centre of its handle. At the top of the handle was the symbol of the Four Corners with the four pairs of hands around the edge. Delicately flipping the key around, he peered at some Roman numerals inscribed on the handle, around the edge of the green crystal.

"I think it says," said Jack squinting closely and trying hard to remember what he had learnt from one of Miss. Turnbull's lessons. "One, two, three, two, six and a five."

"Once I caught a fish alive..." chanted Martin, laughing. Jules flashed him a scornful stare.

"Judging by our past experiences with anything to do with the Four Corners, I strongly believe these numbers will be some form of clue," suggested Jules, carefully taking hold of the key. "No, actually Jack, I think you've got it wrong."

"And I agree," said Holly.

"How can you agree with her? You've not even looked at the numbers yet," defended Jack.

"I know," said Holly breezily. "But if it's a case of who's right between you and Jules...?" No one argued with that.

"Have you both finished?" said Jules, tapping her foot impatiently on the floor. "It's a four, the last number is definitely a number four. The numbers are: one, two, three, two, six and finally *four*."

"That's all well and good," commented Jack testily, "but what do the numbers actually mean?"

"Was there anything else with the key that might give us some idea?" asked BT.

"No," said Jack despondently. The one piece of evidence they possessed might be as much use as a chocolate fireguard.

"Well, I still think my rhyme was quite clever as we're

on a boat. Fish...don't you get it?" Everyone just ignored Martin.

"Hang on a minute," said Jack with a second wind of excitement. "I think there's something else on the key."

"Let's have a look..." said Jules, trying to take the key again.

"Right, kids...are you all ready?" called Roger Hunter, who began rattling the door handle. "Why is this door locked and why's Emma sitting out here all by herself?"

Argh! Parents! They always have an uncanny knack of arriving at precisely the wrong moment.

The Grand Entrance

Chapter Ten

Jack was excited as they prepared to leave the ferry, they were about to touch French soil. This would be his first encounter in a foreign land. Having boarded the minibus, Jack slid into his seat and fastened his seatbelt. He was on holiday – at last. But now he had a new challenge ... unravel the mystery of the key and unlock the second secret!

Jack was sitting next to Martin who was busy attempting to master the perfect French accent – with disastrous results. They had plenty of space so why Emma insisted on sitting right behind his seat was beyond Jack. Emma busied herself plotting their route in one of her geography maps – Jack thought she was mad. Jules sat next to Emma, a white cardboard box on her lap her with her head buried in some book about 'a magic doorknob'.

Jack watched Holly slide Hula Hoops, one onto each finger. Then in the blink of an eye he ate them all, heartily munching away the evidence.

BT was on his handheld console designing some new technical gadget that would probably not work properly. Jack smiled at the mental image of BT with a filthy face as another invention blew up.

Frustration quickly replaced the humour as none of Jack's friends appeared remotely interested in the latest mystery. It was now up to him to figure out why Elizabeth

Coldaire, the famous actress, was travelling incognito …
and what connection the box had with the Four Corners
… all the while dodging Russian mobsters and avoiding
one of the world's most wanted criminals.

For a moment, Jack sat and contemplated the problem.
He decided the best course of action would be to call
Roger Gante and hand him the key after all. Then, he
might just be able to relax and enjoy his holiday.

"Just making sure everyone's here," said Roger Hunter,
practically standing on Jack's seat while doing a head
count. "A bird in the hand is worth two on the bus," he
laughed.

Jack groaned.

The ferry doors slowly opened and they were ready to
disembark. Jack smiled. They would soon be in Paris and
then onto Disneyland.

His dad shouted, "You all got your seatbelts on? We're
all set then, Mary. Get ready for blast off…"

"Do you want to see how far away Paris?" asked Emma
leaning forward and showing her map to Jack.

WER-WER-WER!

"Blast and darnation!" cursed Jack's dad. "Ruddy
thing won't start."

The engine rattled, the van vibrated, but it would not
jump into life.

"You wouldn't have had this problem in my day,"
advised Grandad, aggravating Roger further.

"And what's that dad?" asked Jack's mum calmly.

"Reliability! None of this rubbish you get nowadays. Always breaking down. When I was a lad, you had reliability."

"Yes, yes Harold, I'm sure you're right," muttered Roger Hunter as he unclipped his seat belt and climbed out of the vehicle, still mumbling under his breath.

Thud! "Will you stop kicking my chair!" snarled Jack, turning to glare at Emma.

"Sorry! But, it's not my fault," she replied with the innocence of an angel. "There isn't enough room to swing my legs."

"Children, will you behave back there?" snapped Mary, spinning around and unfairly directing her wrathful look straight at Jack.

Another thud hit the back of Jack's chair. With a deep breath, he started counting, 1...2...3...4... His mum would always do that whenever he annoyed her. He just hoped it worked.

Jack wanted to know what his dad was up to, but the bonnet swung upwards, totally blocking his view. Then he heard Grandad offering assistance to which his dad made no reply.

A car horn blared. The sound amplified in the ferry's parking bay. Jack wondered what the problem could be. It was then that Jules pointed out the obvious. *They* were the problem. They were at the front of the queue and were preventing other cars from driving straight off the ferry. Another car beeped its horn.

How embarrassing.

"Looks like some of the wires have been cut," explained Roger, poking his head through the open door.

"Sabotage!" said Martin, his face instantly draining of colour.

"The crooks!" said Jack. An image of Vladimir cutting the wires with his knife raced through his mind. He felt himself begin to sweat.

"But how did they know this was our vehicle?" asked Holly.

"You kids have been drinking too much pop," laughed Roger. "You've gone and given yourselves an overactive imagination. Looks more like some kind of rodent gnawed through them."

"Urgh, I hate rats!" Martin shuddered.

"I agree," said BT.

"Aw. Don't be daft, they're so furry and cute," said Emma.

"She's not kidding either. She's got an albino rat as a pet in her bedroom," explained Holly.

Jack shivered at the thought. He was not sure which was worse, being hunted by the Russian mobsters or sleeping in a room with a live rat. As he turned around, he noticed Jules. She was sitting rather too quietly, her head buried in the cardboard box on her lap. It was unusual for her not to be involved in a mystery. She always had something to say on any puzzle. And normally, she was right.

"Could be they used a blunt knife," explained Holly. "That would give the appearance of an animal chewing through it."

"Calm down! Calm down. The wires have definitely not been cut by some gangster," confirmed Roger before disappearing back under the bonnet.

"When I was a lad, we played cowboys and Indians. I blame all these modern computer games for giving young'uns all this claptrap 'bout villains and sabotage," grumbled Grandad. Although Jack loved his grandad, at times he did wonder what he was talking about.

If it wasn't embarrassing enough to be broken down in the middle of the ferry, almost every person driving around the stationary bus stared. Jack's dad now had a shocking brain wave. Roger was expecting not only Jack, but all his friends to get out and PUSH the minibus. This was the ultimate humiliation!

Help came from an unlikely source. A car full of Liverpool F.C. fans on their way to a Champions League game in Europe stopped to help. In no time at all, the minibus was down the ramp, off the ferry and parked in a car park – they were on French soil.

Jack wished the Liverpool fans would take him with them, or better still, it was his beloved West Ham playing in the competition. He would do anything to get away from the embarrassing calamity and enjoy his holiday.

Jack could only watch in horror. It should have been Jack getting into their car and being whisked off to the

epic football match, not Roger Hunter.
The very cheek!

The Long Gallery

Chapter Eleven

No matter how much Jack tried, he was unable to sleep. Stuck in a broken-down minibus in the middle of the night, he was tired, hungry, and cold. Emma was hyper after drinking the last can of fizzy pop. The normally quiet girl seemed to be on a mission to be as loud and irritating as possible. All Jack wanted was to be left alone and sulk in peace and quiet. His dream holiday was turning into a disaster.

Every so often, Jules would lift her head up from the book she was reading and begin talking to the box on her lap. Jack was glad he did not read much or, he might end up as crazy as Jules. Jules had not been her usual self since they had begun their journey. At the rate she was going, he feared she might end up locked away in a lunatic asylum.

A pair of headlights came into view. Jack tried not to get too excited. The last few times he thought his dad had returned, the vehicles would change direction. This time, the two white lights against an otherwise black canvas headed straight towards them, growing steadily brighter. The car pulled up right in front of the minibus and Roger Hunter climbed out. Jack did not know whether to be happy or miserable at the sight of his dad.

The door opened. "Look who's back," said Roger in an over cheerful voice. "Have you all missed me?"

"No I have not," Jack muttered loud enough for his friends to hear, but not quite audible to the grownups in the front seats. Jack could only stare as his mother flung herself into his dad's open arms. Gross!

Seconds later, Jack's dad made an announcement. Roger had found a local mechanic who could understand English. His dad went on to explain it would take a couple of days for the new part to arrive. The minibus could then be repaired meaning they would be able to salvage the rest of their holiday. A third of their holiday stuck in Calais completely immobilised. At first, that sounded like a complete disaster. Jack jumped out of his seat in protest, but before he could get any words out of his mouth, the real news was unleashed.

For once, his dad made perfect sense and a reluctant Jack was in total agreement. They would all continue on their journey to Paris, his dad choosing to remain behind with the minibus. It was the best news Jack had heard all week.

Jack's dad was still in the process of explaining *Operation France* as a whirlwind of activity broke out. BT gathered all his technical hardware together. Holly vacated his seat too, leaving behind a mound of empty sweet and crisps wrappers – enough to fill a whole bin liner. Emma put on her white padded puffer coat. Jack thought this was hilarious. She looked more like a giant marshmallow. Jules chucked her rucksack over her shoulder and carefully picked up her box.

Half-heartedly, Jack began collecting his things. His mother followed after them all, double checking that they did not leave anything behind. Jack thought she sounded weary.

His dad, who was beginning to look like a bearded yeti from the lack of shaving, explained the taxi driver who had brought him was going to take them to the train station, just in time to catch the last train to Paris. Grandad gallantly volunteered to stay with Roger and keep him company.

"Right then…make sure you've all got everything," snapped Jack's mum, just as he clambered onto the front seat of the taxi. Both he and Martin had been fighting to claim the prized position and after accidentally tripping Martin (on purpose) Jack emerged the victor.

"Here are the hotel tickets," said his dad, handing Mary the foot-long leather wallet he used for all his valuable documents. "The passports, half the euro's and our birth certificates are also in there, just in case…" At that, they both embraced.

Just as Jack was wondering why his dad would bring their birth certificates, his mum turned round and shouted at him, "Jack Anthony Hunter! Stop your tomfoolery this instance and seat yourself in the back." Jack was just about to complain when his mum continued, "I'm too tired for all of this."

He decided on this occasion to concede, because his mum was tired – but only this once. Slowly, he got out and crawled into the rear of the overcrowded vehicle. Crammed in the back with his head squashed against the cold window, Jack closed his eyes in the hope it was all a bad dream.

***

In the blink of an eye, the most uncomfortable journey Jack had ever endured was at an end. His mum paid the taxi driver as they unloaded their belongings. One adult and six children ventured into the unknown.

Wheeling her suitcase behind her, Mary Hunter led the way. Eventually, after asking three different people for directions – none of whom could speak a word of English – they found the ticket office, where they fared no better. Jack watched as his mum struggled with the odd phrase or two she vaguely remembered from her school days. She began with the basics, *"Poly-filler Anglais?"* The ticket man gave her a vacant look. She then tried again with, *"Votre nom nom est le temps?"* only to be met with a similar blank response.

Just as the thought of never getting to Disneyland began to eat away at Jack, Martin, of all people came up with an idea. He suggested using the hotel tickets. If Mary showed the man in the ticket office their hotel tickets, he would know exactly where they needed to go. Jack wanted to laugh, but Martin's ludicrous suggestion actually worked.

A large man, who had been slouched at the rear of the ticket office, drinking out of a bright orange mug, suddenly appeared from a side door with a baggage trolley. As the door slammed shut, Jack noticed a sign on the door written in French. He did not have a clue what it said. The short dumpy man, who sounded like he had a mouth full of marbles every time he spoke, loaded up the trolley with their belongings and set off.

Martin pointed to the man's bottom and began to giggle. The ticket office attendant's navy blue, pin-striped trousers were slipping down his backside showing an excessive amount of his waist which hung over the side of his trousers. The man had such a funny walk. He waddled like a duck and as he pushed the trolley, his bottom swung from side to side. Jack and Martin were still laughing about it when they were on the train and nestled into their seats.

The train juddered into motion. At last! They were safely aboard the train to Paris. Nothing could go wrong. Soon, they would be arriving at their hotel and after some much-needed sleep – Disneyland. The best part about it was that they did not have to travel in the sickly yellow minibus.

Jack was sure both he and Martin would get a roasting from his mum for laughing so loud about the fat man's waddle. But, when he turned around, she was sound asleep which was very unusual. His mum was like a non-stop, tightly wired clock. Her nap meant only one thing; license for fun!

Much to his dismay, a half-hour later, Jack was bored

with being silly. Jules had been sitting with her head in her box, but now she picked up a book and began busily reading. Emma was asleep, Martin was playing with BT on his games console and Holly was staring out of the window with earphones plugged in.

The one chance he had to do anything he liked; Jack was sitting in his seat doing absolutely nothing. Boring! He rummaged around in his pockets to see if he could find any sweets. Nope, sadly he was clean out. That's when his fingers touched something thin, metal, and ten centimetres long. He'd forgotten all about the old bronze key he had found.

"YES!" he cheered.

The key was similar to the one he had found eight months previously. There was no mistaking the symbol of the Four Corners. Only this time, the key's handle looked more like a polo mint with a green crystal stuck in the middle of the handle. It was here that the Roman numerals spanned the edge of the circle marking out the numbers: one, two, three, two, six and four.

Just as Jack was contemplating the significance of the six digits shown in Roman numerals, he made another discovery. Inscribed faintly along its long, slender shaft were more numbers. This time they were not Roman numerals. They were ordinary numbers. It seemed peculiar to Jack that someone would do this unless the numbers had been added at a later time.

Carefully, he read the numbers; 49 then a space and

then 44027. After scrutinising the key even closer, Jack noticed that there was a dot after the nine, which was actually the reason for the space.

A rush of exhilaration coursed from the tips of his toes right to the top of his head. Jack stared at the numbers, hoping for an amazing revelation to jump out at him.

He waited ... and waited ... and waited. Absolutely nothing!

It would have felt fantastic to decipher the puzzle. The others would definitely be impressed. Twisting the key around in his fingers in the hope of a miraculous revelation, he spotted more numbers. This time they started with a 1 then a space. Though when he double checked, there was another dot. The full inscription read: 1.09636. With a mixture of elation and curiosity, he could not contain himself any longer. He had to tell someone.

"Pssst," whispered Jack, not wanting to wake his mum. "Jules, take a look at these numbers on the side of the key?" It was a no-brainer enlisting her help. She was the most likely of his friends to unlock the meaning of the numbers. Jules had almost singlehandedly solved the secret of King Richard II.

"What?" she muttered, her head peering over the lid of her box. "Can't you see I'm busy?"

"Nothing," huffed Jack. Here they were on the brink of something unbelievable. If his friends were not interested, then he would go it alone. He could imagine the headlines: *Jack Hunter defeats Russian mobsters and uncovers ancient riches.* He did not need their help! He stared at the numbers once again.

Seconds later; "Jules… I really do need to show you something," said Jack with more urgency. He could have easily done it all by himself, but on this occasion he decided to be gracious. He was willing to share the glory with his friends.

Jack heard a loud noise – the sound of metal coarsely rasping against metal. The train was slowing down. Just when he was about to get overexcited, Holly burst his bubble. "We shouldn't be here yet. Paris is miles away."

"Give over. What do you know about train journeys in France?" laughed Jack, hoping deep down that he was right and Holly was somehow wrong.

"Do you know what?" said Jules, "I think Holly could be right. Paris *should* be at least another hour away."

"Well, we're obviously stopping at another station. You know what the bus to Burnley's like. It takes all day with all the stupid stops," said Martin.

In principle, Martin made sense. But, it could not be possible for Martin to come up with two great suggestions in one day. Something did not feel right. BT then confirmed Jack's suspicions. "What if it's the Russians that have stopped the train?" he asked.

"But why would they want to stop this train? It's not exactly as if we have anything they want, is it?" laughed Martin.

Conscious his friends knew something was amiss, Jack replied "What?" with a nervous laugh, the key twiddling in his hands.

"The Key!" exclaimed BT pointing down at Jack.

Jack gulped.

"What Russians?" asked Emma, who had awakened in time to hear at least half of their conversation.

The train came to a screeching halt. Fearing he might see Vladimir and Michael standing on the platform, Jack refused to look out of the window. After deciding he was just being silly, he surveyed the multitude of passengers on the platform. Then he saw the large sign fastened to a brick wall.

They definitely were not in Paris. They were in LILLE!

Chapter Twelve

"Lille?" said Jack hoping for an explanation. By the surprise expression on their faces, he realised they were equally dumbfounded. "What're we doing in Lille?"

"Lille isn't on the way to Paris," suggested Emma.

Before anyone could agree or disagree with Emma, a loud commotion began to take place. It appeared everyone was getting off the train. If it was a scheduled stop on the way to Paris, then it did not make sense why everyone would be getting off the train. The ticket inspector slid their compartment door open and began to garble in French.

It sounded like a beehive as everyone started talking at once. For a moment, the ticket inspector just stood there with a puzzled expression on his face, twiddling his very long moustache between his fingers and thumb.

"All charnge!" the inspector finally explained loudly. Everyone immediately stopped mid-sentence.

Half asleep, Jack's mother pulled out one of the train tickets from her bag and flashed it directly under the ticket inspector's nose. Jack watched in bemusement as the man momentarily went cross-eyed.

"Ah oui," he nodded in acknowledgment. "All charnge!" and pointed through the window towards the platform. Before Mary could make any sense of the ticket inspector's announcement, he turned, exited their compartment, and walked briskly along the corridor with the parting shot, "all charnge!"

They quickly began to collect their belongings. Jack could not find his backpack. After accusing Martin of hiding it, which Martin vehemently denied, and his mum, unbelievably, took Martin's side; Jack vaguely recalled not seeing his bag since departing from his dad and Grandad. To his horror, it suddenly dawned on him that he must have left it on the minibus.

Feeling miserable, Jack shivered as they all stood on the platform, their luggage gathered by their feet. He could not believe he did not have any clean clothes until his dad arrived – and that could be days. A blustery, cold breeze whistled through the station. Looking around at his friends, he saw Emma in her ridiculous, giant marshmallow coat, all snug and toasty.

Too tired to think what to do next, an off duty train driver saved the day. Mary showed him their train tickets and he kindly pointed them in the right direction. Just as they stumbled to the right platform, train lights appeared in the distance.

What appeared to be just a regulation changeover did not sit right with Jack. Paranoid the gangsters were somehow responsible; he kept on the lookout for the two Russians. As he boarded the train, a watchful eye scouring the platform, he saw a tall, elegant woman with a fur hat and ankle length fur coat. Although the woman was partly obscured by other passengers waiting to get on the train – and taking into consideration he was extremely tired – he was certain it was Elizabeth Coldaire.

It was two minutes past midnight and the train would be departing in exactly three minutes. With a sigh, Jack slumped wearily onto his seat. He could hardly keep his eyes open yet his brain was wide awake.

Jack's head was pounding, he was starving beyond the point of feeling hungry, his body ached from tip to toe and, his feet were now throbbing. All he wanted was to get to the hotel, crawl into bed, and sleep for two whole days. Adrenalin was a strange chemical. Despite every bad sensation coursing through his weary body, just a glimmer of Elizabeth Coldaire sent him into a state of hyper-consciousness.

Jack was desperate to share the hot of the press news with his friends – but knew he needed to be discreet. Getting rid of Emma would be as easy as apple pie. The tricky part would be thinking up a really good reason to get his mum to leave them on their own. He thought of telling her he had just witnessed a murder. Too theatrical! Maybe he could say there was a fire. Too dramatic! They were giving away free food in the rear carriage. Not imaginative enough. Just when he had hit a brick wall in the excuses department, he lamely turned towards his mum. Today was his lucky day. His mum was sound asleep and, Emma too.

Jack was about to announce his revelation when he

noticed Holly had also fallen asleep. "Here, Martin," he said, "give Holly a shove and wake him up."

Martin's face suddenly lit up brighter than a Christmas tree. Jack realised that Martin would relish the opportunity of bellowing into Holly's ear louder than a jet aircraft going supersonic. "But, do-it-quietly."

With his friend's attention, albeit sleepily attention, Jack spoke in a hushed voice, "I just saw that famous actress get on this train, the one Jules was telling us about." Jack's friends huddled closer to him.

"What famous actress?" asked Holly, letting out a big yawn.

"You know! The one whose posh handkerchief I found. The woman who had the box full of jewels that the thieves stole on the boat, the box that contained the key…" explained Jack without pausing for breath.

"He means," said Jules as both Holly and Martin stared blankly. "Elizabeth Coldaire."

Instantly, he could see the penny drop as they both said, "Oh that woman!" At times, Jack wondered how they had managed to solve the mystery last summer.

"Do you think she's following us?" asked BT, "because I've been reading about how to follow someone wearing the perfect disguise! It's all in my spy book in chapter thirteen. I'd let you have a read, but it's in my bag I left on the bus with my clothes."

"What…you left your clothes behind? Then what's in that large bag you brought?" said Martin, asking the same question Jack was thinking.

"Stuff," replied BT with a secretive smile on his face.

"Stuff? What do you mean by *stuff*?" asked Martin.

"You know...secret stuff," said BT with a cheeky wink.

"Look, this isn't getting us anywhere. What we need to find out is why that famous actress woman is on this train. For all we know she could be trying to follow us," said Jack. "And we need to figure out what the new numbers I found on the key mean. They have to be some sort of clue."

"What new numbers?" asked Holly as he wiped the sleep out of his eyes.

"Oh, I never got chance to tell you, did I..." realised Jack. "I've found a load of different numbers etched along the length of the key," he said excitedly.

"Coolio!" grinned Martin. "Can I see, can I?" Martin was now jumping up and down on his seat like a mad ape.

"Martin, be quiet!" hushed Jules, "Otherwise, you'll wake..." And she pointed to Jack's mum. Martin threw himself onto his seat with a thud and crossed his arms defiantly. "The key sounds interesting, but we can look at that later when we get to Paris. As for Elizabeth Coldaire, a lot of films are made in Paris; there are even movie studios just like in Hollywood. So it's no big deal she's on this train. You're just getting paranoid," explained Jules.

"No I'm not. You sound like my mum and dad. They didn't believe me last year and it turned out I was right.

I might not have all the answers like you. But I can tell when something is a bit weird and I'll prove you wrong – even if I have to do it alone," huffed Jack, shoving his hands in his pockets and walking towards the carriage door.

"Wait... Jack, I didn't mean it like that," defended Jules.

"Hang on, guys," interrupted Holly. "Jack might be onto something here. If Elizabeth Coldaire is on her way to Paris and a top movie star feels the need to be travelling around on a train in the middle of the night and not flying there in a flash jet, then why did she not get on this train in Calais?"

"That's right," said Jack enthusiastically, turning back from the door. "This proves she must be following us."

"Well, it doesn't actually *prove* anything other than she's trying to travel in peace for once, away from the relentless pursuit of the paparazzi," said Jules, not convinced.

"That's 'cause she would've had to switch trains like us," said BT. Jack was deflated, they were now back to square one.

"I think we should try and find her," suggested Martin, eagerly.

"I agree," said Jack.

"Well in that case," said BT, standing in the middle of the group and cracking his fingers, "step aside and let the master do his work."

"Who says *you're* the master?" asked Martin sarcastically.

"Because...I've read all the spy books," exclaimed BT, folding his arms.

"Just because you've read a few books, doesn't mean that you're better at it than me," said Martin, squaring up to BT in the middle of the carriage.

"Okay then, ignoring the fact I know everything about international espionage, have you got a sneaker-phone?" challenged BT.

"A what?" asked Martin.

"Or have you got refracto-glasses?" asked BT.

"Refractoid what?" asked Martin, even more confused.

"Exactly my point! They're super spy glasses that I've invented which means you can look around corners and see if there's anyone hiding before you get there. They use a special infrared frequency that bounces the images back off all the walls, displaying a 3D image. If you haven't got the equipment, then you'll never be a proper spy," said BT.

Martin opened his mouth to argue, but quickly closed it when no words came out.

"Listen to yourselves, you two...just stop it. We're never going to get anywhere at this rate. Our only realistic option is to split up," explained Jules firmly.

"Well, I'm not going with you," replied Martin, "or him," wagging his finger at BT.

"Then you can go with Jack," ordered Jules.

Without further discussion, the two parties separated. BT, Holly, and Jules set off together in one direction. Wearing his special refracto-glasses, BT took the lead. Jack watched in amusement as BT stopped four feet short of the end of the carriage corridor, crouching down he inched forward like a duck with a limp. With that vision in mind, Jack turned and jogged to catch up to Martin who was already marching in the opposite direction.

The plan was simple: Whichever group found Elizabeth Coldaire would leave at least one person to tail her while sending someone back to inform the rest. The fact that Jules had come up with the plan would normally annoy Jack. He wanted to think of all the best ideas. On this occasion, all he really wanted to do was sleep.

Jack and Martin travelled through carriage after carriage without any sign of the actress. It was very late and Jack could hardly keep his eyes open. He was desperate he would be the one to find the movie star.

Just then, the train inexplicably shook. Off balance, Jack grabbed hold of the nearest seat to steady himself. Martin was not so lucky and tumbled onto a huge woman who looked like a bossy hospital matron, his face landing on her sizable and sloping chest. Miraculously, she remained sound asleep, but her arm swung round and grabbed Martin, pulling him even closer. All Jack could see were Martin's legs wriggling like a worm. With a sigh of disbelief, Jack grabbed one of Martin's trainers and carefully began to pry him away from her slumbering grasp. After a few seconds tussling with the giant woman's vice-like grip, Martin emerged from the ordeal, hair sticking out in every direction and his face redder than a beetroot. Jack wanted to laugh, but the distraught look on Martin's face stopped him.

The train's overnight lights flickered off momentarily pitching the train into complete darkness. As the light returned, the train juddered again. This time, Martin made sure he grabbed hold of a headrest to prevent himself from falling over.

They slid open the door at the end of the carriage and entered into a long, narrow corridor. The walls were made from tarnished steel and there were no windows. It looked like they had searched the last passenger compartment.

"Where are we?" asked Martin, the first time either of them had spoken since his embarrassing misfortune with the large woman.

"Dunno," replied Jack.

"Is there much point carrying on? She isn't gonna be down here. Looks more like this area's for staff. And it feels sort of... Creepy!"

Although Jack agreed with Martin, he desperately wanted to be the one that found Elizabeth Coldaire. "Let's just try the door at the end. If we don't see her, we'll go back," said Jack.

As they reached the far end of the empty corridor, the lights flickered off again plunging them into darkness.

Unable to see anything, Jack listened hard. The only noise he could hear was the faint hypnotic sound of the train wheels clattering along the track. Something brushed against Jack's leg and he let out a faint scream. The lights pinged into life. Martin was stood right by his side.

"You stupid idiot, why are you standing right next to me?" defended Jack. He did not want to look like he was scared, especially not in front of Martin.

"It was all a bit eerie, and I thought if I stood near you–"

"Never mind any of that. Come on, now," commanded Jack, cutting Martin short, portraying a confidence he did not feel.

He tried the handle to the door at the end of the train carriage. It did not want to move. "It's locked," explained Jack.

"Here, let me try," said Martin, confidently brushing past. There was a click and the door slid effortlessly open.

"I loosened it," said Jack sheepishly. Martin grinned.

A solitary light bulb hanging on a wire barely lit the carriage, the corners of the room remaining in shadows. From what Jack could make out they were standing in a storage compartment with crates and boxes stacked everywhere. Sawdust littered the floor and metal chains hung down from the ceiling. Jack was just stepping around a large wooden crate tall enough to fit a baby giraffe inside, when the light went out. Unable to see, he knocked his elbow against something. It took all his effort not to yelp in pain.

The light bulb fired into life again. There, standing in front of Jack was a very, large man.

The first thing Jack noticed was a tattoo of a snake down the side of his face.

"Arggh!" he howled.

"What's up?" asked Martin.

The light went out again. Jack quickly inched backwards, away from the sinister looking man. Sweat was pouring down his body and he could feel himself go all goose-bumpy.

"Ouch!" shouted Martin. "Somebody stepped on my foot."

The light came back on. Jack did not want to look at the man, but his eyes could not help but stare. The man stood motionless, his eyelids closed.

Jack backed away a little further. That's when he looked at the ground and wished he hadn't.

The man's feet were dangling six inches off the floor. Looking up, he noticed that there were chains wrapped tightly around the man. That is when a voice inside Jack's head connected the dots.

The man was dead!

"R-u-n!" screamed Jack, his voice trembling with fear. He tried to run backwards, only to trip over Martin, sending the pair of them crashing to the floor. The two of them scrambled madly to their feet. In the darkness,

Jack caught his foot in a coil of chains. He fell again.

Martin was the first to the door, but for some reason he did not open it. Jack crashed into the back of him. "Hurry u-up! Op-pen it!" He was sure he could hear something – or someone – moving behind them.

"I can't…the handles stuck. It won't move!" cried Martin, firmly grasping the handle with both hands and tugging at it with all his might. Jack leaned against the door and tried to help Martin slide it open.

The lights flickered again. The sound of shuffling behind them was growing louder. Jack's heart beat like a drum at the thought of what may be creeping up behind them. He wished he was off the train and safely tucked up in his hotel bed.

The two of them heaved at the door. Suddenly, the handle clicked and the door slid open. Caught by surprise, they began to fall. This time, they both managed to keep their balance, and they ran as fast as they could along the metal corridor.

Without stopping, Jack reached the door at the far end of the carriage and opened it as fast as he could, Martin by his side.

Whack!

Jack and Martin had hit something large – and firm.

Bouncing off the obstruction, they both flew in the air before landing on their backsides.

"Watch where you're going," a disgruntled man snapped at them.

At first, Jack looked at the man's scruffy shoes. Then he glanced upwards to see a tubby man in a double-breasted grey suit. His gaze moved slowly until his eyes met the man's annoyed expression. That is when Jack received a second shock.

"Er, I-In-spect-tor Gante...?"

"Jack Hunter?" Roger Gante M.I. (to be precise), stood in the doorway looking more surprised than Jack. "What on earth are you doing here?"

"I'm-erm, going on holiday," explained Jack, saying the first thing that entered into his head.

"No! No! Not *that*! I meant, what are you doing here, running around the train like two wild beasts from Borneo...and at such a late hour?" Roger Gante clarified.

"Uh," Jack paused. He did not know what to say. He had no excuse, no plan. He was clean out of ideas. "There's a dead body down there, sir," said Jack clambering to his feet and pointing towards the cargo compartment, his arm shaking.

"A dead body? Don't be ridiculous… Are you sure?"

"Yes sir. Honest. It's just in that room there," said Jack with a little more confidence.

"Let's go and take a look, shall we? But this had better not be a silly childish game!" Roger Gante said as he strode ahead. Jack and Martin hesitated a moment before quickly scurrying after him.

The man from Interpol operated the handle with ease and slid the door aside. The solitary light bulb dimly lighting the room was working. Roger Gante proceeded to pull an object – that looked remarkably like a gun – from within the folds of his jacket.

Jack gulped.

"Now then, where did you say this dead body was?" said Roger Gante in a hushed tone.

Cowering behind the Inspector, Jack pointed beyond the uneven stack of crates.

Inspector Gante stepped forward. Jack remained rooted to the spot. Martin lingered in the doorway.

With his gun cocked and poised for action, Roger Gante disappeared behind the crates.

A split second later, he reappeared, sliding his gun back into its holster, concealed behind his suit jacket.

"I think you boys had better get back to your seats before I arrest you for wasting an International official's valuable time."

Jack's jaw fell to the floor. He had definitely seen a man's dead body, with a tattoo of a snake on his face to prove it. On the other hand, he did not want to be arrested.

Silently, both Jack and Martin skulked back to their compartment. They slid the door open to be greeted by Jules, BT, and Holly. That is when Jack noticed his mum sat wide awake, her face like thunder with her arms crossed. Before Mary could scold the two boys, Roger Gante appeared in the doorway.

"Mrs. Hunter?" he enquired.

"Can I help?" she said, sounding full of cold as she wiped her nose with a paper tissue. "Is there a problem?"

"Perhaps, if you wouldn't mind stepping out here," suggested Roger Gante leading the way. "And perhaps we could discuss the matter in private."

Minutes later, Jack watched in horror as his mum returned and closed the door behind her, a look of annoyance blazoned across her face.

"Jack Anthony Hunter," his mum stood with her hands on her hips. "You're in serious hot water. I cannot believe I fall asleep and that you can't be trusted to sit here with your friends and behave for one, single minute."

It was not Jack's fault. He had witnessed a murder – well sort of – he had found a dead body ... and the grownups were only bothered about punishing *him*. It was a travesty of justice! Before he was able to protest his innocence, the train suddenly braked.

At last, they had arrived, sparing him from any further chastisement. He hoped that when the following morning arrived, his mum would have either forgotten why she was annoyed, or she would have calmed down enough for him to work his charm.

Everyone began to grab their possessions. Jack was desperate to find out if the others had found Elizabeth Coldaire. His mum was too close to BT and Holly, while Jules was sticking her head back inside her cardboard box. No wonder everything was going wrong. His friends needed to have their heads in the game, not stuck in boxes. Jack would just have to ask later.

Jack looked out of the window into the dark night. Lights on the platform lit up the station as the train slowly ground to a halt.

At last they had arrived, safe and sound in ... "ROUEN?!"

The Inner Courtyard

Chapter Thirteen

The following morning, Jack awoke with a pounding head. He had hardly slept. Trying to figure out what happened that night was like swimming through pea soup.

The confusion had started when they arrived at Rouen. His trusted mum would normally be on hand to sort out the mess and save the day. However, she was not herself and struggled to muster enough strength to stay on her feet. In the end, after getting into trouble on the train, Jack decided to take control of the situation in the secret hope of regaining his mum's favour.

He figured Rouen must be like King's Cross Station or Liverpool Street Station in London. If his memory served him correctly, there were four train stations in London. (He knew this from playing Monopoly!) None of them actually said *London*. So he reckoned that Rouen must be the name for one of the main train stations in Paris.

Although wobbly with fatigue, Emma informed them that Rouen was nowhere near Paris. According to her, it was actually in the province of Normandy. Jack did not know who Norman was, but what he did know was a sleep-walking eight-year-old girl made no sense. In the end, he told her to mind her own business.

The taxi had taken them straight to their hotel, *The Hotel De Paris*, where they were shown immediately to their rooms.

Score: Jack one; everyone else, *nil.*

Climbing from his bed, Jack pushed open the drab, pastel blue curtains. Light flooded into the room, hurting his eyes. He did not have a clue what time of day it was. He was hoping to see the Eiffel Tower or, better still, the turrets from Disneyland towering majestically over the city. To his dismay, all he could see was the building opposite, which was not very picturesque.

Looking around the room for the first time, Jack slowly absorbed his new surroundings. It was very basic with three double beds and a few bits of furniture. All his friends were still asleep. Jules was sharing with Emma, Holly with BT while he had the unfortunate pleasure of sharing his private space with Martin who had wriggled like a worm all night.

Their accommodation was not very holiday-like. Jack had envisioned marble staircases leading up to his room with a four-poster bed all to himself and a balcony that overlooked all the best parts of Paris.

There was a door between two of the beds that led into the hotel room next door. At least it meant they had some privacy from the adults. Jack peered around the door to see his mum still sleeping.

Jack was fed up. As a result of the incident on the train, his mum would not allow Jack out. The good news? The others could not go to Disneyland without an adult and as his mum felt too ill to leave the hotel, Jack's sentence became easier to swallow. That was until he discovered Emma would also be staying. If only he could find a way to escape the room and ditch Emma.

"Watch out for the giant rats," mumbled Martin as he lay sleeping. Martin had a real phobia about rats. Jack laughed at his friend writhing around under the covers, no doubt having a nightmare. The dilemma of waking Martin and putting him out of the misery or leaving him to suffer his rat infested nightmare meant at least Jack's own problems faded to the very back of his mind.

Jules was the first to rise. She looked funny in her white pyjamas with pink rabbits dotted over them. Jack laughed again. She strode across the bedroom with a toothbrush and toothpaste tube in one hand and bottle of shampoo in the other, scowling at him.

Still glaring at Jack, she slammed the bathroom door behind her. The loud bang was enough to rouse the rest of his friends from their peaceful sleep. Martin jumped so high, Jack thought he might actually hit his head on the ceiling.

"Where's my flies?" said BT sounding irate.

Poking her towel-covered head out of the bathroom door, "Oh, they were yours?" said Jules, a layer of white foam surrounding her mouth. "I threw them away." She then disappeared back into the bathroom.

"What!" protested BT. "You can't do that, they're not yours. What you done with 'em?"

"I expect they're on their way to the tip by now in the

bin wagon. I mean, what a stupid thing to keep in a jar. Whoever heard of someone collecting flies? It's just… umm," she mumbled as she continued to brush her teeth. She closed the bathroom shut and the bolt could be heard sliding across in its lock.

"But they weren't *real flies*! They were spy-flies, for my sneaker-phone," pouted BT.

Making their way downstairs for breakfast, the argument over personal possessions continued to blaze in the hotel reception. Apparently, every single one of BT's spy-flies had taken hours of work to create, not to mention the cost. The spy-flies contained two miniature cameras, one concealed in each eye, enabling a near perfect 3D image to be relayed back to his phone. The arguing only stopped when they started eating.

Jack was not impressed with the food. The croissants tasted like cardboard. A young waitress called Mia, who could speak near-perfect English, sneaked Jack a slice of toast spread with Nutella.

His friends now began talking about exploring Paris. They did not seem remotely bothered he was not allowed to go with them. Discovering the whereabouts of Elizabeth Coldaire or uncovering the meaning of the numbers on the ancient key would have been a much better use of their time.

"And don't you think it's strange that Elizabeth Coldaire just disappeared?" asked Jack, hoping to stimulate some enthusiasm from his friends.

"I bet she wasn't even on the train," said Holly, wiping a smudge of leftover strawberry jam from the side of his mouth and licking it from his finger.

"What do you mean? Of course she was! You calling me a liar?" flared Jack, jumping from his seat.

"Calm down! I'm not calling you anything," said Holly mildly. "Just saying that you were the only one... ummm...who saw her on the boat and then, you were... ummm...the only one who saw her get on the train," explained Holly, stuffing a third jam covered croissant into his mouth.

"I did!" protested Jack, slowly reclaiming his seat. "She was real, just like the dead body that me and Martin saw. And that vanished too!"

"Well…" said Martin sheepishly, "I didn't actually *see* the dead body." He shrank down into his chair.

"What do you mean, you didn't see it...you were there...it was right in front of us!" spluttered Jack.

"Well, either the light was out, or you were blocking my view, or I was being knocked to the floor," shrugged Martin, shrinking further into his chair.

"I can't believe you're all doing this," exclaimed Jack. "It's like you're conspiring against me. That's it..." Jack jumped to his feet, almost knocking his chair over.

"What do you mean by that...?" gasped Jules.

"No, you're too busy talking to boxes. They'll be taking you to the funny farm next," snapped Jack and stormed off before she could reply.

***

Jack sat on his bed, his arms wrapped around his raised knees. The prospect of being stuck in the hotel room *all day* was not his idea of fun. He was supposed to be on holiday.

He held the ancient key, twiddling it between his fingers, staring blankly at the numbers over and over again.

"Do you want to look at my book?" asked Emma who was sprawled on the floor in the middle of the room. "Geography's fun."

"Just great!" muttered Jack.

It was amazing how Emma was a girl clone of Holly. "I'm busy," he said, ignoring her.

"No you're not," she replied matter-of-factly. "You're just sitting there."

"I'm busy, er...thinking."

"What you thinking about?"

"About nothing," he said. Her inquisitive nature was getting on his nerves.

"You can't think about nothing," she observed. "It's impossible."

"Alright," huffed Jack, knowing technically she was right. "I'll look at your book with you." Before he could move, she was bouncing on the bed by his side.

Her book was actually a homemade scrap book with various styles of maps glued onto its pages. There were numerous grid lines and lots of numbers. She had even drawn some of the maps herself. He figured she must be mental – just like her brother Holly – wanting to waste all her spare time on cartography (he only knew the proper name because she had told him – more than once!). Jack was surprised at the quality of the maps. Some of her drawings were impressive. She had real talent! Not like him. Jack's greatest skill seemed to be upsetting people.

"So this is where we are in Rouen," she said pointing to the top of one of the pages. "And this is Paris, all the way down here." Jack watched as her finger moved down the page until she stopped where the letters PARIS were marked.

It did not make any sense. She had to be wrong. They were staying in a hotel with *Paris* in its name. The hotel tickets were all in order.

"What are those numbers there?" he asked.

"Which? Those ones there?" said Emma pointing to one of the grid lines. "That's the longitudinal reference number and this here is the latitude. With both numbers you have the geographic coordinates for any location on the planet. See? I told you this was fun."

"Do you have a pen and piece of paper I could borrow for a second?" Jack asked her.

Excited, Jack rushed into the bathroom, making sure the door was locked before carefully taking the key out of his pocket. The last thing he wanted to do was show Emma the key. Quickly, he scribbled down the two sets of numbers inscribed along both sides of the key. Heart racing, he burst into the bedroom.

"Here…" he asked, handing her the piece of paper. "Are these numbers geographic-cor-di-whatsits?"

"They could be," said Emma. "They do look exactly like them."

"Can you work out where this location is then?" he asked, his voice trembling with anticipation.

Their hotel room door suddenly swung open. "Martin, you goon…watch what you're doing," shouted Jules as Martin barged his way into the room.

Jack was bursting, desperate to tell them his news. As it turned out, his friends had news of their own.

The Kitchen

Chapter Fourteen

"You're never going to believe it, Jack!" shrieked Martin, waving his arms around like a windmill.

"Yeah, guess what we've found out?" added BT.

"We're not in Paris," said Jules, calmly removing her bag from her shoulder and hanging it on the door handle.

"Yeah, it turns out we're in a city called, Rouen!" added Holly, looking dorky in a brown stripy tank top.

Before Jack could get a word out, the four of them surrounded him as he sat on his bed, all talking at once making it almost impossible to understand a single word they were saying. His ears were beginning to hurt from the muddled noise.

In the hurry to broadcast their important news, his friends had forgotten to shut the door. Jack was shocked to see someone outside their hotel room, eavesdropping. A strange looking figure in a hooded robe was definitely showing abnormal interest in *their* business. As Jack made eye contact with the hooded figure, the man fled.

Jumping from his bed, Jack rushed past his bemused friends. "They've got Jules' handbag!" he shouted before disappearing out into the hotel corridor. Looking left then right, he spotted the figure climbing through an open window at the end of the corridor.

"It's got my money and my passport in it!" screamed Jules, distraught.

"Quick," called Jack to his friends. Racing after the hooded figure he reached the open window in time to see the thief clambering down the fire escape. If Jack hoped to save Jules' bag, he needed to think quickly.

"That's the person who keeps following me and he was listening in on our conversation outside the door and now he's taken Jules' bag," explained Jack.

"But why would someone–?"

"Never mind that now. They're getting away," interrupted Jules, pointing through the window towards the fire escape.

"Well, I'm not climbing through that window, or down that rickety ladder," said Holly. Jack was already racing back along the corridor. Reaching the elevator, he repeatedly pressed the button.

The five of them crammed into the small lift. Jack pressed the bottom button marked 'S'. He didn't know what the French word for 'ground' was, but figured the bottom button always represented the ground floor no matter which country you lived in. The lift was so slow! Jack wondered why, whenever he was in a rush, everything always took twice as long.

The elevator door opened and they pushed the metal concertina gate out of their way. First out of the elevator was Jack, charging across the small lobby of the hotel and through the double doors onto the street, his friends lethargically in tow. Jack looked up and down the road. A few parked cars lined the street. People were walking on both sides of the pavement, but there was no sign of the person who had snatched Jules' bag. A noisy red Citroën drove by interrupting his concentration.

"There…" pointed Martin. Jack followed Martin's outstretched finger in time to see the man running across the street.

"Come on," shouted Jack. The five of them ran across the road. Another Citroën car, this time a bright blue one, narrowly missed them. They reached the safety of the pavement just as the car horn blared at them.

The thief rounded the corner at the end of the street. Running as fast they could, Jack and his friends chased the man. They were gaining on him.

Disaster struck. The thief jumped onto the back of a waiting moped. Jack could only stare as the little engine, sounding more like his mum's hairdryer, revved into action.

"My bag!" sobbed Jules, sure it was gone for good.

Outside a local grocery store, a scruffy dog tied to a signpost barked. Leaning against the shop front were three bicycles. Before Jack could think of their next move, Martin had scrambled onto one of the bikes. At first, Jack watched in horror. A vision of Martin clapped in irons with two French policemen dressed in blue uniforms marching either side of him flashed through his mind. Holly too, darted for a bike and set off along the pavement, nearly knocking into a man more preoccupied with reading his paper than watching where he was walking. Finally, Jack sprang into action, barely beating BT to the last available bike.

Martin and Holly were already in hot pursuit. Jack pedalled as hard as he could to catch up. He was riding a bright pink ladies' bike. It only had three gears that were operated by a flick control on the handlebars, right next to a brass bell. Every time Jack tried to change gear, he accidently rang the bell. It was highly embarrassing.

Jack was just catching up to his friends when a loaf of French bread hit him on the side of the face. "What the flying cats is going on?" muttered Jack, rubbing his head.

He heard a cry from Holly. "Look out!" A tin of snail soup hit his handle bars, ricocheting over his left shoulder as he ducked. Jack looked ahead in the direction of the flying food. Martin had picked the best bike except for one minor detail, a shopping basket on the front, which was loaded with food. Unable to see past the mountain of groceries sticking out of the basket, Martin began discarding the food.

The moped was pulling away. As long as it remained in sight, they had a chance. Ahead, the road turned sharply to the left. The person who snatched Jules' handbag disappeared around the bend.

A supersize box of cereal hit Holly's back wheel. Jack suddenly found himself in the middle of a cornflake shower. Trying to wipe a couple of the crusty cornflakes out of his eyes, he was too late to dodge a flying head of lettuce.

Whack! The leafy green projectile hit Jack squarely on the head, temporarily dazing him.

Jack lost his grip, causing the front wheel to spin out of control. He was heading straight for a parked car. At the very last second, he regained control, steering it up a curb and onto the pavement, narrowly missing the car.

Then he saw a stone wall. Heading straight for a tall stone post Jack clenched his eyes shut. Twisting the handle bars as hard as he could, he managed to swerve, missing the upright post by millimetres. Jack only briefly averted crashing. Before he could slam on the brakes, he found himself shuddering and jolting violently as the bike hurtled down a steep flight of steps.

"Look out!" he shouted to an innocent couple holding hands. They were forced to jump apart as Jack steered his bike right through the middle of them. Jack looked hastily back over his shoulder. He spotted the man's feet wiggling furiously. Wedged upside down in a hedge the rest of his body was hidden from sight. The woman stood shaking her fist at him. The one time when he could have used the bell for its intended use, Jack forgot it was there. "S-s-sorry!" he shouted through chattering teeth.

The bike's bumpy trip down the steps convulsed through Jack's body as every bone was being shaken to pieces. He felt like a spaceship breaking up on its attempt to enter earth's atmosphere. At the rate he was going, he would not survive re-entry. The wheel dropped down another step causing his chin to bang onto his chest.

"Ouch!" he howled as he bit his tongue.

The bike hurtled off the last of the stone steps, only to careen into the road. A horn blasted loudly. Jack looked up just as a moped carrying two people whizzed past. By sheer fluke, he had taken a shortcut and caught up to the bag snatcher and accomplice. There was no time to examine for broken bones. Just as Martin and Holly appeared around the corner, Jack kicked down hard on the pedals on the girly-pink bike and set off in hot pursuit.

Riding downhill meant Jack was able to catch his breath. But it also meant the thief was slowly pulling away. No matter how hard Jack pedalled, he could not close the gap. The purse snatcher was going to get away and there was nothing he could do about it.

Suddenly, Jack heard a whooshing noise. He stared in disbelief as something flashed past him at an alarming speed. At first, he could not make out what it was. It was just a blur. It definitely was neither a car nor a bike. Then he saw sparks flying out from its... Shoes?!

Half in shock, Jack stopped pedalling and came to a standstill. Seconds later, Martin and Holly braked alongside him.

"Did you see that?" gasped Martin.

"What...puff...was...puff...that?" panted Holly, slouching over his handlebars and as red as a beetroot.

For a second, Jack could not reply. He thought he knew the answer, but his brain would not process the information and relay it to his tongue. "I think," Jack finally said, "that was BT."

"What? But how?" gasped Martin in disbelief.

"Turbo shoes," shrugged Jack.

The Dungeon

Chapter Fifteen

BT whizzed after the moped across a busy junction, running a red light and disappearing into the mayhem of rush hour traffic. Jack wondered whether jumping the lights on turbo shoes was actually considered breaking the law.

Desperate to know what was happening, Jack, Holly and Martin waited for over ten minutes. When BT still did not return they decided to make their way back in the hope he had gone straight to the hotel with Jules' bag.

Jack wished they would fit escalators onto steep hills. Puffing and panting, struggling to gain any momentum, he looked down at the bike. The front wheel was bent out of shape and numerous broken spokes stuck out at all angles.

Slowly pushing the three 'borrowed' bikes up the hill, they trudged towards the grocery store. Cresting the brow of the hill, they spotted a bustling crowd gathered ahead.

"BT must be back after recovering Jules bag and they're cheering him," observed Martin.

"Don't be daft…" wheezed Holly, slouching over the handle bars. "There's obviously a very good musician playing for money outside that grocery shop."

Pushing the bicycles, they made their way toward the

growing mass of people. Jack spotted a small police car mounted on the kerb. An animated woman with fiery-red hair and matching apron was complaining loudly to the policeman emerging from his car. A barrage of heated words was audible. Someone in the crowd suddenly pointed towards Jack and shouted in French.

"Oh no!" gulped Jack. "I think we're in trouble."

"What for?" asked Martin, in innocent surprise. Before Jack could explain the obvious, the short woman in the bright red apron waddled towards Martin. She snatched the bike out of his grasp. Wagging her finger, she spat at him like a furious cat. A blond-haired man in his early twenties laid claim to the girly pink bike Jack had been riding. When he saw the damage Jack had caused, he went into a fit of rage. Jack had never seen anyone turn that shade of purple before.

A baying mob quickly surrounded them. People shouted in angry tones, shaking their fists accusingly – Jack could not understand a single word. One little girl who looked to be only five-years-old came up to Jack and kicked him on the shins. The two police officers stepped in between the crowd and the three boys. Slowly Jack – still rubbing his sore shin – and his friends were ushered towards the police car, before the irate mob threatened to break out of control.

The three boys were soon crammed into the back of the rather tiny police car and on their way to freedom. This was Jack's first ride in a police car and hopefully his last. The policeman driving the car turned the radio on. The foreign music was terrible. It screeched worse than a choir of wailing alley cats. The car drove around the corner and along the street to their hotel. Jack was impressed that the two police officers did not miss a trick. They even knew which hotel the boys were staying in.

As Jack stared out the window, he was sure he spotted BT walking towards the hotel. But a green truck with a picture of a giant tomato painted along its side, which Jack presumed was going to the grocery store where he had borrowed the bike, drove past, momentarily blocking his view. Jack hoped fidgeting on his seat would make the truck move out of his view faster. Finally, he saw BT sauntering along the pavement. He appeared to be whistling, his head bobbing merrily and he was carrying something under his arm – Jules' handbag!

There was no opportunity to rejoice in their triumph while they were crammed like prisoners in the back seat. The car drove to the four-storey, cube-shaped building. However, instead of stopping outside the front door, the car drove straight past.

"Whoa..." exclaimed Jack in alarm. "That's our hotel over there. You've just passed our stop."

The police officer in the passenger seat turned around, an irate look on his face. His expression made him look more like a farmyard animal than an officer of the law. Simply shrugging his shoulders, he turned up the radio.

"You can't do this," squealed Martin, his voice sounding more like a little girl than a boy of nearly thirteen. "We have rights, you know. We're British citizens!"

The two policemen simply ignored their pleas to be let out of the car and began talking to each other. In England, they would have received a slap on the wrist and advised to behave in the future. But, this was France. Their rules, Jack imagined, must be a lot tougher. He pictured himself being thrown into a dark cell.

When Jack thought he heard one of the policemen mention rhubarb crumble, he relaxed a little. At least if they were going to be served apple and rhubarb pie with custard in prison, it would not be too bad. A low growl from the depths of his stomach suddenly reminded Jack that he had not eaten since breakfast. Now he wished he had eaten that extra slice of toast.

The police station was nothing like he imagined. Instead of being bundled into a cold, damp, prison cell, they were escorted into a compact room with only one solid wall. Dozens of maps were attached to the wall with coloured pins. This masked the awful interior decor. Perfectly straight lines drawn in black marker crisscrossed the maps. It looked exciting. The other three walls were made entirely of glass panels and he could see right into a bustling police station.

They were seated on an uncomfortable red sofa, barely big enough for the three of them. All he could feel were the springs. It reminded Jack of sitting in a chair at his

Aunt Meredith's, which he once had to endure for a whole sunny Saturday afternoon. He remembered it well because all his friends were at the park playing football, while he was stuck indoors on that uncomfortable chair. Afterwards, he could not walk properly for nearly a week. Jack tried to focus on the memory, but could not remember why he was there. He was now forced to place his hands under his bottom just to make it more comfortable. Then the fattest man he had ever seen entered the room.

"So then... Tut, tut... What have we here?" asked the policeman who spoke very good English. "My, oh my, this just won't do. I have enough trouble trying to keep down local crime as it is without having to deal with silly pranks like this. Now, this may be common practice in England. But, in France, I can assure you, this is simply not acceptable," He wheezed as he ranted, his cheeks glowing as red as a post box.

He continued pacing up and down with his hands behind his back. "My, oh my…" the policeman sighed.

His trousers were so big, Jack reckoned that he, Martin, and Holly could fit inside them and there would still be room to spare. The man was not wearing a jacket and Jack could see his trousers were held up by a pair of braces, the elastic fraying along the edges – most probably from the immense strain.

There was a long pause. Jack was not sure whether to speak or remain silent. The policeman had not asked a direct question. Jack was scared to say anything, in case it was recorded and later used against him.

Just as the man opened his mouth to deliver his verdict, a knock at the door stopped him. With a sigh of relief, Jack followed Martin and Holly's lead and turned towards the door. His heart sank as none other than Roger Gante poked his head into the room; "Can I have a word?" he directed the question to the large policeman. The officer closed the door with such force, some of the maps fluttered violently in the draught.

Before the boys had chance to conspire, the door opened again and Roger Gante stepped in, alone. Jack feared the worst. "Can you please tell me what happened?" he asked, calmly. For a second none of them spoke. Then just like someone had pressed their start buttons, they simultaneously broke into chatter. "Okay! Okay!" ordered Roger. "That will do! Now then," he said, "one at a time, if you please." Jack looked at Holly, who in turn, looked at Martin. Martin turned to face Jack, throwing him a very blank expression. It was down to him, *again.*

For some reason, Jack began to explain the events backwards. Starting at the end seemed the most logical thing to do. So he told Roger Gante all about driving past the hotel where they were stopping, the journey in the police car, and the angry mob. All the while, Jack could not take his gaze off the man's scuffed shoes. Shame and embarrassment prevented Jack from looking

Roger Gante directly in his face. The one time he let his guard down and looked up, the man just rolled his eyes.

In Jack's mind, there were only two options available, either be arrested and miss their holiday, or face the wrath of his mum. From where he was sitting, a few days locked in a cell eating rhubarb and custard seemed by far the better of the two options.

It wasn't until he got to the part of his story when he described the thief's appearance that Roger Gante stopped him short. It was a shock to find out the man from Interpol was actually listening to his story. It was even more surprising that he was taking Jack seriously.

"These hooded characters are part of a criminal fraternity headed by George Martin," the man from Interpol announced. Jack inwardly laughed at the thought of a criminal mastermind having a name like Martin. "And it appears...he thinks you have something that belongs to him. Do you?" he asked sternly.

Nervously, Jack shook his head from side to side. He was not lying, because the key did not actually belong to George Martin. It belonged to Elizabeth Coldaire. Then a strange thing happened. Roger Gante apologised for mistrusting Jack on the train.

"It appears to me that all is not well and you unfortunate souls have gotten yourselves caught up in the middle of whatever's going on. I shall arrange for an officer to give you a ride back to your hotel and, I suggest you stay there. If you do have to go out, make sure you keep your eyes open. Whatever you do, do not wander off on your own. Do you still have my phone number, Jack?" the Inspector asked. Jack nodded. "Very good. If you see anyone looking suspicious, please don't hesitate to call me. We have our net closing in on George Martin as we speak. It's only going to be a matter of time. That slippery eel won't elude me any longer. I *always* get my man." Spinning around on his heel, Roger Gante opened the door and spoke to someone, in French.

As they left the police station, Roger Gante called after them, "Please remember, you have nothing to worry about."

"Nothing to worry about," hissed Holly in a shrill voice, as they travelled in the back of the police car. "Nothing to worry about? Is he mad?"

"I thought he was alright," said Jack. "At least he believed us and wanted to help."

The policeman driving them back to the hotel was busy singing along to the radio. "But what good is help if we're dead?" continued Holly quietly. "You should have given him the key."

"No! I think you're overreacting," said Jack. "He said I could phone him at anytime." Jack pulled out the fancy card with Roger Gante's contact details on, waving it around proudly as though it were made out of solid gold.

"You're not getting it, are you? This George master criminal person is wanted by Interpol. He works with Russian mobsters with guns–"

"Knives," corrected Jack. "Those Russian gangsters only had knives. Well, actually, it was only one knife."

"That's not the point, is it? In the end, the result will be exactly the same. And he's got people in creepy looking hoods who have not only managed to track us down, but they're following us around. Do you actually think, 'There's nothing to worry about'?"

The debate raged on until the car pulled up outside The Hotel de Paris. The policeman – who did not speak a single word in English – escorted them as far as the elevator, making sure they were safely inside before leaving them alone.

Martin continued to argue his point. Finally, the elevator stopped at their floor with a bump. Rushing out, Jack ran to their hotel room and opened the door. BT and Jules were stood waiting. Although he was happy to see them, Jack sensed something was wrong. Jules tried to throw her eyes sideways as if to say something. Unfortunately for Jack, he did not understand eyeball language.

There was someone else in their room.

The two of them parted. Mary Hunter was waiting patiently, sitting on his bed with folded arms, tapping her foot.

"And where the blazes have you been?" she demanded.

Chapter Sixteen

"I'm fed up to the back teeth…"

Sitting with his head bowed, Jack tried unsuccessfully to switch off his mum's nagging voice. He vaguely heard a few words break through into consciousness – his mum had tried ringing his dad … phone dead … Dad driving all over Paris … stuck in Rouen … all Jack's fault. She was almost hysterical.

"Wharrrt?" shrugged Jack innocently, wearing an angelic expression that would convince even the Pope!

Miraculously, things did not end too badly. After the initial fire and brimstone from his mum had subsided, Jack found out Roger Gante, of all people, had phoned his mum to explain everything. The Inspector assured Jack's mum that both he and his friends were blameless.

Thankfully, the rest of the conversation faded into 'blah…blah…blah'. Just at the point Jack hoped his holiday could finally get back on track, his mum stood, wobbled, and immediately collapsed.

Not knowing what to do, Jack raced down to the reception to get help. With tears welling in his eyes, he was relieved to find Mia at the reception desk. She could speak good English and understood what needed to be done. She immediately phoned for a doctor.

The doctor seemed to take an eternity to arrive; when he did, Jack wondered if he would be much use. Dressed all in black, the frail, gray-haired man looked so frail that the slightest gust of wind could snap him in two. Even his immaculately pressed, three-piece suit gave the impression that the doctor was already prepared for his own funeral.

***

Jack made sure his mum was tucked up safely in bed. The doctor then pulled Jack to one side to explain that his mum had a fever and he would return later with her medication. In the meantime, he advised Jack to make sure his mum got plenty of rest. The doctor suggested she remain in her bed where she could be left in peace and quiet for at least a couple of days. From the doctor's grave expression, Jack could tell what he actually meant to say was; *Away from all you noisy kids.*

A pan full of worry for his mum's well being mixed together with a whole jar of responsibility, left Jack swimming in a stew of confusion. The doctor had barely left when Jack's mournful, worried daze was interrupted by yet another crisis.

"Arghh!" screamed Holly, standing at the far end of their hotel room. He was foaming at the mouth, his lips blackening. Alarmed, Jack immediately thought Holly had contracted some form of disease.

"He's been poisoned!" shouted Martin in a panic. An image of a hooded man spiking their food with poison flashed into Jack's mind.

Holly's face was now turning purple. Jack could only

watch as Holly shot past him, running towards the bathroom, hands clasped around his throat and spitting furiously. "Get me a drink…" he demanded, weakly. Jules quickly rushed to his aid looking whiter than a ghost.

The fog began to lift in Jack's mind. Thinking clearly he knew exactly what needed to be done. He was just about to open the door and chase after the doctor. The physician was so old and dithery that Jack figured he could only have made it to the end of the corridor.

With his face slowly returning to its natural colour, Holly reappeared from the bathroom.

"What was all that about?" asked BT, bemused by all the commotion.

"I've been poisoned! That's what's happening," explained Holly, pointing to a small pile of raisins on top of the cabinet next to his bed. "I thought them foul things were chocolate covered raisins."

"They look nothing like chocolate covered raisins," said Martin, stating the obvious.

"Not English ones!" conceded Holly. "But we're in France and they eat all kinds of different stuff…don't they? And besides, I thought room service had left them there to nibble on. You know, like the mints at reception downstairs."

"What? There's free mints downstairs in the lobby?" asked Martin, surprised.

"Well, there were, but someone ate them all," said

Jack.

"You mean he ate them all," said BT looking accusingly at Holly, whose cheeks began to turn crimson, again.

"It wasn't my fault. We've hardly eaten properly for days and I'm dying of starvation," said Holly innocently, tugging at his jumper and showing the excess material hanging loosely around his waist. "Anyway, don't you try changing the subject; have a bit of respect for my tender condition. I've just been poisoned, haven't I?"

Martin was about to speak again, but Jack jumped in first. "Well, if they're not French raisins, what're they?" Looking to Jules for an answer, he was surprised to see her standing sheepishly by the bathroom door, awfully quiet. She usually had an explanation for everything.

"What's up with you…cat got your tongue?" remarked Martin snidely, pointing at Jules from across the room.

"Lola!" shrieked Jules, causing everyone to jump. In one movement, she leapt across the room, diving under one of the beds and almost disappearing from view. All Jack could see were Jule's stripy-socked feet wriggling about underneath the end of the bed.

"Lola? What she going on about Lola for?" asked Martin, puzzled.

Jules emerged from underneath the bed. She was not alone. As she clambered to her feet, snuggling in the safety of her arms was Lola, her fluffy pet rabbit. A flood of realisation washed over Jack. Her random and weird behaviour of talking to herself and sticking her head inside the box she had been carrying now made perfect sense.

"What did you have to bring that flea ridden thing for?" demanded Martin, marching across the room, pointing at the rabbit.

"Never mind her rabbit…what about me? I've nearly been poisoned," Holly continued to remonstrate.

"It's not my fault! I didn't have a choice because Samantha Pepper promised to look after her, but then she came down with chickenpox. So I had to bring her along. If I'd left her at home with mum doting over Reginald, she would've probably starved to death by the time we returned home."

"What a stupid thing to do. Why would we want that here with us?" demanded Martin. Jack sensed an argument about to explode between the two siblings. Thankfully, Holly prevented World-War-Brown from erupting, although, he also sounded unimpressed by Lola's uninvited appearance.

"Hang on a minute," he said. "If your rabbit's been running around this room, then does that mean those raisin things I ate are…? Urgh! That's so disgusting!"

"Ha-Ha, Holly's been eating rabbit poo…do-dah, do-dah," chanted Martin, skipping round the room in delight, completely forgetting his grudge with Jules.

It took a few minutes for the chaos to settle down. Jack was itching to continue solving the mystery. Before he was able to tell his friends his news, Emma entered the room. She had been sitting with Mary while she rested in bed, showing her one of her handmade geography scrapbooks.

There was a slight groan as she joined them, especially from Holly. While Jack and his friends had been busy with regular, everyday occurrences – like chasing after the hooded thief, or cooling their heels down at the police station – Emma had figured out the numbers on the key. A hush fell over the room as her amazing revelation sunk in.

"If it wasn't for the fact that you were my sister," laughed Holly at hearing her news, "I would have said you were a full-blown-genius. But then, I'm the only genius in our family." His friends gave him a disbelieving stare.

Chapter Seventeen

Several hooded figures surrounded Jack. They were closing in. Where were his friends? He caught a glimpse of one of the figure's faces. Fear seized him. This was not a man, but a creature ... half flesh, half skull ... a solitary, fiery, piercing red eye. Jack was trapped. He felt something strike him on the side of his face. Pain seared across his face.

Jack felt a claw scratch at his face. He sat up streaming with sweat. The fearful creatures with burning eyes had been nothing more than a bad nightmare. Just then, something landed on his face. He nearly leapt out of bed. The creature was warm and furry... Lola.

Forcefully shoving the rabbit away from him Jack jumped out of bed. He could not understand why Jules had brought her one-eyed rabbit, let alone allow it to roam freely in their hotel room.

"Alright then, mate? You ready for the big exploration?" said Holly, already up and dressed.

Now Jack was even more confused. Without warning, a small man inside Jack's head opened a door, allowing streams of light to flood into his foggy mind. Multiple images flashed before his eyes as realisation dawned upon him. They were on holiday in France, but in the wrong town. His mum was ill and his dad was lost – the thought of his dad lost gave Jack a momentarily happy thought!

Jack then recalled Emma's clever deciphering of the numbers on the old key that had inadvertently come into their possession. They were on the trail of a new mystery, a new historical secret. It was all beginning to fall into place.

Then something nagged in his thoughts, although there was an element that seemed just a little too convenient, almost engineered. According to Emma, the two separate numbers along the shaft of the key were actually the longitude and latitude references. What should have been an exciting discovery now worried Jack. The location the key indicated was none other than the **Cathedrale Notre Dame de Rouen**, simply known as Rouen Cathedral. Surely, it was too impossible a coincidence that they ended up in Rouen.

When his dad had ordered the hotel tickets online, it could have been purely coincidental that he picked the Hotel de Paris. Jules pointed out that Jack's dad could easily have mistaken Rouen for a suburb of Paris. The error was complete as soon as Roger Hunter assumed that a hotel with Paris in its name would be in…well, Paris! Still, Jack had reason to be cautious. He had already crossed paths with Russian mobsters. Plus one of the world's most notorious criminal masterminds had been chasing him, and that was all before he stumbled across a dead body that inexplicably vanished into thin air.

"But why not?" whined Emma. "It was me that figured out the keys secret in the first place."

Emma had a valid point and Jack felt guilty when he again said, "No," He watched the tears well up in Emma's eyes. "It's too dangerous," he tried to console her by explaining what they were up against. "I'd never forgive myself if anything happened to you," he said, sounding just like a grownup. "And besides," he added lamely, "we need someone to look after my mum and Lola."

"That's right," added Holly, happy to ensure his younger sister was kept away from the adventure. "That's an important job too, you know."

"It's for the best," said Jack, convincing his friends they had made the right decision as they stepped into the hotel's elevator. "If George Martin is somewhere out there in Rouen, then the last thing we want to do is put an eight-year-old in that kind of danger."

By the time they reached the lobby, the decision to leave Emma (and the rabbit) behind had been completely forgotten. Next stop... Rouen Cathedral. They were embarking on a new adventure – that is until Holly threw a spanner in the works.

Holly pointed out that if the numbers were longitude and latitude references, they could not be as old as the key because those references were not invented until the eighteenth century. They must have been added to the key hundreds of years later, which would not tie up with the dateline of The Four Corners. What did Jack care whether Holly was right about the numbers? They were on a new adventure, a chance to find more buried treasure.

Jules then came up with a great theory. The Four Corners had been a very powerful order that included among others, Emperors and Kings. So it could be logical to assume they invented longitude and latitude hundreds of years earlier than was now believed, but kept it a secret. That way, they would have the ability to cross the world by sea without having to worry about any interference from their enemies.

Whenever Jules came up with an idea, the others rarely contested her. She was always right – to the point of being downright annoying at times. On this occasion, her hypothesis meant they headed towards Rouen Cathedral with a renewed spring in their step.

It was a bright, sunny day. Jack caught a glimpse of his reflection smiling back at him as they passed a tailor shop whose windows were practically bare. A small bespectacled man, wearing a dark blue waistcoat with a tape measure slung around his neck, suddenly poked his head around the side of a threadbare tailor's dummy, causing Jack to jump.

Jack quickly switched his gaze to an odd looking fancy dress shop with a couple of mannequins standing in its window. One was adorned in a cowboy outfit, the other dressed in a red and white striped shirt and black beret.

With no sign of life inside, it was hard to determine whether the shop was open for business. The faded red woodwork was in dire need of a fresh coat of paint. Large areas had simply flaked off with the passing of time and neglect.

The next shop along the parade was derelict. Numerous posters advertising an array of events were pasted over every inch of the empty shop. Although in French, Jack recognised one was promoting a circus, purely because it had a picture of a brightly coloured big top tent.

Just then Jules stopped dead. "I don't believe it..." she gasped, pointing towards one of the posters. "Elizabeth Coldaire! It's a picture of Elizabeth Coldaire."

"Okay, now this is really starting to freak me out. First of all, the key Jack found just happens to lead us to Rouen and now there are pictures of the mysterious film actress, right here as well," said BT, sounding unusually spooked.

"Not only that," Jules continued, "but I think this poster is advertising that she's performing in a sort of theatrical production, right here in Rouen at the **Theatre de la Chapelle Saint-Louis.**

"But why would a world famous movie star be in some sort of local production in this small town?" puzzled BT.

"I wouldn't say Rouen is exactly a small town, but I do get your point," said Holly in an unusually non-sarcastic manner.

"Whatever. It just all seems too much of a coincidence.

I don't like the look of this at all," said BT, throwing his hands up in the air. Jack was in total agreement with BT. However, he was too curious to simply do nothing. He had to find out what it was all about.

"And the weird thing about this play, I think it's just for one performance and, it starts in half an hour," said Jules.

"Wow, that's amazing. I didn't think you could read French. How did you do that?" asked Jack.

"Probably using a French dictionary," yawned Holly.

"Actually, it's written right here at the bottom in small writing which is in English," said Jules pointing to the poster again. "If you took the trouble to lift your head out of your stuffy old history books once in a while, then perhaps you might spot the obvious."

"Way to go, sis..." cheered Martin. "I wouldn't bother with a comeback after that slam-dunk, mate." After slapping Holly on his back, Martin gave Jules a high-five.

"It's all well and good acting childish," said Holly, "but if it starts in half an hour, then we'd better get going." At that, Holly turned away and set off briskly down the street.

"Oh, Holly..." Jules called after him. "According to the small map on the poster, I recommend you try going more in that direction." Trying hard not to laugh, she pointed to a path partially hidden between the end of a terraced house and the boundary wall of a small church.

Five minutes later, they were standing outside the theatre, the small disagreements forgotten. For a venue boasting a guest performance from one of the world's most famous stars, Jack thought it looked – well – ordinary.

It was left to Jules to order the tickets on the basis she was good at everything. Although she tried to argue that she could not speak French, Martin, Holly and BT pushed her forward. Jack was too busy staring at the outside of the building. It seemed like they had built the theatre the wrong way around, starting at the roof and finishing at the ground. There was the obvious stamp of architectural genius in parts, particularly the stone work ornately arched at the top, but as they got to the floor, it was as though they had run out of creative juice. An image of a brilliant, yet crazy French, master stonemason stood on his head was erased from Jack's mind by Jules stumbling out of the theatre's entrance and bumping into him with the bad news – they were not allowed into the theatre without adult supervision.

"Typical French bureaucrats," mumbled BT. "Don't they know my father invented the sneaker-phone by request from the head of the French Secret Service?"

"It's pointless arguing. If there's one thing I've learned over the years from my study of medieval Anglo/French relations, it's that the French don't really like the English," explained Holly, stating the obvious. Even Jack could have told them that they were wasting their time without dragging up another history lesson.

"Ooh-la-la-la!" squealed Martin.

"Ooh-la-la-idiot," mimicked Jack, pointing his finger towards his own head and twirling it around in circles. "I think you've gone a little ooh-la-la."

"It was a bilingual expression of brainius...!" explained Martin. Everybody else, including Jack, stared at Martin in disbelief.

"There's no such word," said Holly.

"It's a cross between genius and brainy. So do you want to hear my plan, or not?" Without giving his friends chance to reply, Martin continued. "I watched in this film once where they managed to stand on top of each other in disguise. No one could see right through it and at the end, they got the chocolate for free as well."

"If there's free chocolate...I'm in," said Holly, patting his stomach.

"What're you babbling on about?" queried Jack.

"Come on! I'll show you." Martin grabbed Jack by the wrist.

Leading them back in the direction they had just come from, Martin took them to the steps that ran between the end terrace and the church wall. Landing at the bottom in one giant leap, he turned to face the others, arms outstretched as if to celebrate scoring the winning goal in a cup final. Bemused and out of breath, Jack leapt the last few steps.

"Ta-dah! We're here then," said Martin with a smile

so wide, you could fit a coat hanger inside. Turning around, Martin pointed across the road. They were back on the street where they had seen the poster advertising Elizabeth Coldaire's performance at the theatre.

"Well, what is it?" wheezed Holly finally catching them up. "This had better be good..."

"Don't you get it?" asked Martin surprised.

"No," said Jack, Jules and Holly, all at the same time.

"Yeah, yeah...I do. Its genius," agreed BT.

"Get what?" said Jack still puzzled.

"The fancy dress shop!"

Jack could see there was a fancy dress shop and did not need reminding of the fact. He remembered seeing the cowboy outfit in the window and wondered how that could help their predicament. Martin went on to explain his plan. They could hire a man's coat and hat, so they could pretend to be a grownup visiting the theatre with his children.

"It's the dumbest thing I've ever heard," said Jack. "They'll see right through it."

"I don't hear you coming up with any ideas of your own. It's our only chance, and besides, it's *you* who wants to crack this wide open," said BT.

"I know, but that was before Martin suggested Holly sitting on my shoulders. It's going to be me that cracks wide open. Why can't I be the one that gets to be on top?" growled Jack.

"We've already been through that once... *Because*,

Holly looks the oldest and you're the only one strong enough to lift him up," said Jules. Jack definitely did not agree.

"It's only for two minutes until we get inside," explained Martin. "Then once we've got past the guy in the ticket box, you can act normal." Jack was sure he saw Martin smirk.

"We've been in enough trouble as it is," protested Jack. "If they call the police, it's my mum who'll go hurricane," said Jack, worried his words were simply falling on deaf ears. "And then I'm gonna be the one that cops it."

Several failed attempts later at trying to convince his friends that the plan would never succeed; Jack was stuck with Holly on his shoulders. The problem was not a case of Holly being fat, because he wasn't. He was simply... big. Jack's knees crumpled as Holly hoisted himself up onto his shoulders. "You're so h-e-a-v-y," groaned Jack.

"I'm bigger than the average bear," quipped Holly, which did nothing to help Jack, struggling with the dead lump on his shoulders.

The coat was thrown over the top of them, immediately it was as though someone had switched the lights off. With one hand grasping Holly's legs, Jack parted the front of the coat and looked at their reflection in a car window.

"We're doomed..." moaned Jack. Their disguise would not even fool a fool.

"Hush Jack," said Jules, forcing Jack's head back into

the coat and fastening the buttons.

Sweating inside the coat, Jack staggered forwards, buckling under Holly's substantial weight. He was sure they would be caught red-handed and turned over to the police.

Two minutes later, a tall and peculiar looking man, wearing a long, grey duffle coat – which would appear odd to any person who happened to pass by on that lovely spring day – sporting a ginger beard and wearing a trilby hat that only partially covered his bushy ginger locks ... approached the ticket office of the Theatre de la Chapelle. Three children – two boys and one girl – scuttled along by the man's side.

Unable to stop under the momentum of carrying a baby elephant on his shoulders, Jack ran into something and hit his forehead. He let out a subdued groan through clenched teeth.

"Whoops, sorry there," he heard Holly speak in a deep voice. "Can I have set une tickets for la show...?" Jack wanted to bury his head in hands. This could not get any worse. "Eine erwachesen..."

"That's German," Jack heard Jules whispering from behind. He could swear he could hear the police sirens already. "Erm sorry, I meant set une adulte and trios enfants," said Holly. Then, after a long pause he added, "Merci."

KER-CHING went the cash register.

Jack felt Holly's knees kicking him into life like a race

jockey. He was not a horse! Slowly, Jack reversed before wobbling forwards again, heading safely in the direction of the auditorium.

Just as they got to their seats, the lights were dimming – the show was about to start. Jack could not walk another inch. He happily collapsed, sending Holly tumbling into the aisle in front. Thankfully, the theatre was pretty empty.

"Set une tickets?" said Jack, no longer just the legs of a six-foot-six-tall, ginger bearded man. "What were you trying to speak in French for? You sounded like a complete ape."

"Well, I thought I sounded convincing," protested Holly. "Besides," he pointed out, "we got in didn't we?"

"Shush," hushed a voice from the row behind.

Embarrassed, Jack slunk down into his seat. Before he was able to focus on the play, the thought of the Russian mobsters entering the theatre took control of his imagination. As the show played onstage, an alternative performance acted out in Jack's mind.

An elbow in his side interrupted Jack. He had just eluded a bald Russian swiping at him with a big knife while taking out three of his accomplice's with a single punch. "What?" he moaned, rubbing his sore ribs.

"She's on now. Look," said Jules excitedly.

For the first time, Jack focused his attention towards the stage. A car made from boxes pulled up outside the backdrop of a mansion and Elizabeth Coldaire, dressed in an elegant, flowing, white sequin dress stepped out of the fake car. A chorus of singing butlers danced onto the stage dismantling the car. The boxes became suitcases as the butlers carried them through the doors of the mansion.

This is the stupidest thing I have ever seen, thought Jack. *Whoever heard of a car that turned into suitcases?* It wasn't surprising that the theatre was half empty. Looking back towards the stage, he watched Elizabeth Coldaire gracefully glide across the floor. Within seconds, Jack was mesmerised.

The side lights came on signalling the end of the show. "Is it half time?" quizzed Jack.

"We're not at a football match," said Jules sarcastically. "And for your information, the show has finished."

"What...already?" exclaimed Jack, furrowing his brow, confused. "That went quick."

"So what do we do now?" asked Martin leaning forward.

The main lights burst into life creating a feeling of daylight inside the auditorium.

"It's simple," said BT, "we just follooo–"

"Que faites-vous?" a loud voice bellowed. Jack knew it was directed at them. Sure enough, before he could turn around, an usherette stood at the end of their row wagging her finger. *There was something about the French and waving their hands about in the air*, Jack told himself.

"Sortir aujourd'hui! Sortir aujourd'hui!" she shouted,

her face screwing up like a walnut shell. She began pushing her way along their aisle and forcing them out of their seats. Jack stumbled into the centre aisle. They were being ushered in the direction of the main stage. To the right was an insignificant red curtain with a poorly illuminated green sign above. The woman steered them to the exit. Desperate to get away from the scolding usherette, Jack rushed past Martin, pushed back the curtain, heaved down on the metal bar across the door and swung it open. Now Jack would never get to question Elizabeth Coldaire.

As Holly tripped over the threshold, the door slammed shut behind them, the woman's grating voice still reverberating in Jack's ears. They were in a dirty looking alleyway – the sort he would not want to visit in the middle of the night for fear of being attacked by gangsters or zombies. Looking like the Leaning Tower of Pisa, a pile of disused wooden pallets leant against a large skip overflowing with rubbish.

"She only threw us out because them two had taken off their disguise," said Martin pointing unhappily towards Holly and Jack.

"So what do we do now?" said BT, kicking an empty can lying in the alley.

"Well, the front of the theatre is just up there," pointed Jules. "I suggest we go and wait outside, until Elizabeth Coldaire appears...and then we follow her." Jack thought Jules plan sounded simple – but good.

"But what if there's a car waiting for her outside, or better still, a Hummer limo. We'd have no chance of following her," argued Martin. Jules gave her brother a stare so cold, it could turn water to ice. Suddenly, Jules plan did not seem so foolproof after all.

"That's easy," smiled BT, "we hail a cab like they do in the movies and ask them to tail her."

The plan was back on track.

They walked to the front of the theatre and peered round the corner. Then they hit a major problem. They had gone the wrong way. For once, Jules had been wrong. They suddenly found themselves at the *back* of the theatre. A small squabble erupted over whose fault it was. Still quarrelling, they set off back down the alleyway – only this time in the right direction.

As they approached the emergency exit they had been so mercilessly bundled out of minutes earlier, the door unexpectedly swung open. As quick as rabbits, the five of them shot behind the large bin overflowing with waste. It smelled terrible.

Martin trod on Jack's foot as he tried to force his way to the front, hoping to get a better view. Clasping his hand over his mouth to prevent himself from howling with one hand, Jack swung back his elbow and with a perfect shot, hit Martin in the jaw. A large smile spread across his face as Martin's agony eased the pain in Jack's throbbing toes.

The stench coming from the refuse was so bad Jack

had to pinch his nose and hold his breath, both at the same time. After a minute, he peered cautiously around the edge of the tall bin. To his surprise, he saw Elizabeth Coldaire. She was not alone. Two men were with her.

Jack nearly swallowed the mint he was sucking. The taller of the two men had a bald patch. Jack would recognise them both anywhere. They were the two mobsters he had briefly seen from behind the cocktail bar on the ferry.

Unaware of the gangsters' presence, his friends jockeyed for better positions behind him. One false move, an accidental trip or kicking an empty can and the two Russians would be on them in a flash. Jack could not tell if they were having a friendly chat about the weather, or threatening her life. He ducked back out of view, more bothered about protecting his friends than what the three adults were discussing.

The sound of a glass bottle being kicked alerted Jack that someone was approaching. He turned to face his friends and tried to signal to them with eye language to be extremely quiet and still.

Vladimir and Michael came into view. Jack and his friends were done for. All he could picture was the large knife in Vladimir's pocket. If Jack and his friends were to end up as sushi, no one would ever know.

Jack was afraid he could not hold his breath any longer. The two men waltzed straight past them without batting an eyelid. They had not even noticed Jack and his friends. The gangsters disappeared around the corner at the end of the theatre. Jack gasped for air before trying to explain to the others what he had witnessed. "They ... boat ... Russians," he garbled. The others threw him puzzled looks. "From the boat ... the men with the box ... two gangsters ... Elizabeth Coldaire," he explained with slightly more coherency.

"No way," whistled Martin.

"We haven't got time to waste," said Jules, jumping off an old car battery she had been forced to stand on. "Elizabeth Coldaire is getting away."

"What about the gangsters?" said Holly, a faint tremble to his voice.

"We'll take care of that," said BT immediately grabbing Holly by his sleeve and dragging him into action. "I've still got one spy-fly left." Off they ran in the same direction as Vladimir and Michael.

For a split second, Jack stood and watched BT and Holly run off on their deadly mission, unsure what BT's plan entailed.

Suddenly, Jules barked out orders. Elizabeth Coldaire was getting away. It was the jumpstart Jack needed. Jules, Martin and Jack began to run in the opposite direction in the hope of catching Elizabeth Coldaire up.

When they reached the end of the alleyway, there was no sign of the movie actress anywhere. Frantically, they scoured the busy street. They would have to split up once again.

"There!" shouted Martin grabbing Jack by the shoulder. The most famous person Jack had ever met emerged from a small newsstand.

Jack wanted to ask why a top movie star was wandering through the streets of Rouen, incognito and alone, but there was no time to waste. They dashed into the middle of the road after her. A beeping horn and the screech of burning rubber caused Jack to turn around in horror. Without looking, Martin had simply run straight out in front of a taxi.

Thankfully, he was unhurt.

There was no time to hang around and apologise to the driver. Jack could still hear the man's angry voice shouting in the distance. They rounded the corner where Elizabeth Coldaire had disappeared moments earlier.

"I can see her," shouted Jules quickening her pace.

"Hold on a minute," said Jack. "We don't want to get too close. Otherwise, if she turns around, she might realise we're following her. We'd better cross over to the other side of the road. That way, if she does look around, she won't notice us. We need to act casual." It wasn't often Jack came up with a good suggestion, but when he did, he was brilliant (or so he thought).

To the untrained eye, they looked just like three regular kids, sauntering along the street, out for a pleasant stroll, minding their own business. "Don't you think we're overdoing this casual walking bit a little?" said Martin. "This skipping stuff is more for girls and to be honest, I feel kind of...silly!"

Daylight was slowly beginning to fade. A cold breeze caused Jack to shiver. Their target looked right and then left before ducking down a narrow snicket in between two tall buildings. They crossed the road and shot after the movie star, mirroring her every move.

Apprehensively, Jack stepped into the narrow alley. Darkness quickly enveloped them causing an feeling to wash over him. What trouble was he dragging his friends into? Would he see his mum again? What was he thinking? He needed to be back at the hotel to take care of her!

A screeching cat landed near Jack, and he almost leapt into the air.

"Shush," whispered Jules sharply as she spun round, her index finger firmly placed against her lips.

"It's not my fault," complained Jack, kicking an empty crisp packet lying harmlessly on the ground, relieving his frustration. "That stupid cat gave me a fright." It wasn't until the words left his mouth that he felt a bit dumb, especially telling a girl he had been scared. "But only because I wasn't expecting it," he added, squaring his shoulders to convince her he was tough and it all had been a silly misunderstanding.

In the lead, Martin took the next left. They found themselves walking across empty wasteland that led to an apparently unused factory. The large pipes stretching across the old warehouse ceiling cast strange shadows as the sunlight disappeared.

"What was that?" Jack asked his friends in a hushed voice.

"What was what?" said Jules, looking around in every direction, worry etched across her face.

"I thought I heard something behind us."

"It's just in your head, mate," said Martin sarcastically.

The echoes of Elizabeth Coldaire's stiletto heels clacking over the concrete floor could be heard from the far end of the derelict building. She was getting away! Jack turned and sprinted after her.

It was difficult to run through the empty warehouse. Old machinery and broken debris were scattered everywhere. If only they had a torch. Jack figured if BT were there, he would have had at least one torch at the bottom of his rucksack. The thought of BT made Jack think of his friends, he hoped they were safe. Although one of the Russians carried a big knife, Jack knew that BT was the one friend who could take care of himself. He never failed to have a technical gadget for any situation.

Too busy watching Elizabeth Coldaire and not watching where he was walking, Jack stepped on a pane of broken glass. Elizabeth Coldaire stopped. He watched in horror as she glanced back over her shoulder.

Quick as a flash, Jack ducked down behind a metal oil drum. He was annoyed with himself for being so careless and hoped 'operation surveillance' had not ruined. In the quietness that followed, all he could hear was his own heavy breathing.

"What you doing, lying down there?" bellowed Martin, shattering the silence, completely oblivious to the fact they were supposed to be spying on the actress and needed to be discreet.

"Shush, you idiot. You'll give us away! Now get down quickly before she sees you," hissed Jack, trying to remain quiet so Elizabeth Coldaire wouldn't realise she was being followed.

"But there's no one there," shrugged Martin, allegedly pointing towards an empty space.

Getting his breath Jack lifted his head over the top of the rusty oil drum, peering into the darkness. There was just enough light to realise there was no sign of the movie star in the empty warehouse.

"What're you two messing around at?" grinned Jules as she walked smartly past. Stepping through a gaping hole in the wall, she entered another room before adding. "Well, come on then, we haven't got all day."

Jack remained crouched behind the safety of the metal drum watching Jules make her way across the second room in the warehouse. Martin nudged Jack before running after Jules. Not wanting to be left behind Jack jumped into action.

The three of them headed for a half open door at the far side of the ghostly room, Jules leading the way. She was the first to the door, pulling it open. But, before she had chance to enter, Martin and Jack came running up behind, jostling her in the back. All three of them made it through the open doorway at the same time.

They entered a small white room. A solitary light bulb hanging from the ceiling swung from side to side. There was something strangely unsettling about the room. Then Jack noticed there were no windows or any other doors.

"Are you sure she came through *this* door? There's no way out!" said Jack. "Martin...what you doing?" asked Jack, confused. Martin was standing at the far wall twiddling a round wheel.

"I think this must open a door," replied Martin, absorbed in his attempts to exit the room.

"Martin," snapped Jules. "How many times do I have to remind you...not to mess with—"

Before either of his friends could say another word, Jack felt the floor melt away from under his feet, as if a trapdoor had just opened. Before they realised what was happening all three of them were sliding down a slimy, wooden chute. The air around them instantly became ice cold.

The journey along the steep slope into the darkness only lasted a split second. Then a small light suddenly appeared. Before Jack knew what was happening, he was no longer whizzing along on some sort of slide, he was falling through midair. As they fell, Martin managed to kick Jack in his ear.

SPLASH!

Martin and Jack disappeared underwater. Gasping for air, Jack's head emerged, just as another loud splash suggested Jules had crash-landed a few feet away. The stench was terrible. Martin's head resurfaced above the water like a freshly cast fishing float.

"Urgh!" spat Martin. "This water tastes foul. I got a right mouthful of it."

"Can't you ever leave stuff alone," said a disgruntled Jules. She was soaked through and covered in slime. "You just can't help yourself, can you? Always messing with things that don't concern you. You just had to go and touch something...didn't you?" ranted Jules. Jack thought she was never going to stop.

"But I–"

"Don't give me that. If there's ever a button marked DANGER – DO NOT PRESS, I could bet a million pounds that you would press it."

"I was only trying–" spluttered Martin.

"That's your problem, you just never think...do you?!"

"I–" protested Martin.

"And what is that awful stench?"

Jack was not listening to his friend's petty argument. For starters, his ear still throbbed after having been kicked by Martin and he was also busy, trying to piece together what had just taken place. They were in some sort of large copper waste disposal tank. The sides of the copper wall were illuminated by a light coming from a small window near the top of the tank. From what he could see it was the only exit, their only way out.

A light flickered from the window and Jack was positive he saw someone peer through the opening. Elizabeth Coldaire? He wondered. She seemed to look straight at him. Then she was gone!

"Did you see that?" asked Jack while trying to remove a piece of slimy gunk stuck in his hair. "*Elizabeth Coldaire* was just up there looking down at us. She must have known we were following her and led us here...into this trap!"

The Great Hall

Chapter Eighteen

Crouching down near the end of the alley, BT un-zipped his rucksack. Rummaging around the bottom of his bag, he finally touched what he was after and pulled out his refracto-glasses. The glasses were an aid to see around corners to prevent being spotted which he had invented. "Come on slowcoach," urged BT, "they're getting into a car, we're gonna lose them."

"Wait up," puffed Holly, using his hand to lean against the side of the wall. With a quick intake of air, he pushed himself upright before chasing after BT.

A dark-coloured saloon car with blacked-out windows pulled away from the back of the theatre. Seconds later, BT was standing in the space vacated by the car. He began waving vigorously at an approaching taxi.

"Do you speak English?" asked BT, climbing into the back of the car.

"Ahh, you are from England...Oui? I have er...a cousin named Jean-Luc who lives there...Jean-Luc Mason. He's very good man. Do you know him?"

"No," said Holly, struggling to fasten his seatbelt.

"Follow that car!" commanded BT with an air of authority.

"Ahh, we play James Bond. I love Monsieur Bond." The taxi driver laughed as the car jolted into action. He pulled out seamlessly and slotted into the flow of traffic.

BT spotted the black car ahead. Within seconds, they were losing ground on the Russian's. This was supposed to be a high speed chase, not a Sunday outing.

A dogged determination not to let the two gangsters get away overtook BT. He did not want to let his friends down. "Step on it!" he ordered the cab driver, pointing to the black car they were following.

"Leave it to Francois," the cab driver bragged. "I know every short cut in the city..." Before BT could catch Francois' last words, the car swung sharply to the left, sending Holly tumbling on top of him. BT couldn't breathe, Holly was smothering him. Much to his relief and another turn later, Holly went flying across the back seat, hitting his head against the passenger window. As if in slow motion, BT watched Holly's contorted face slide down the glass.

"No, no, no!" admonished the driver. "You should have put your seatbelt on my young friend. Er, how do you say it...clunk-der-le-click," chuckled Francois.

"I'm trying," said Holly in desperation, his face turning crimson from bouncing about on the back seat. Holly was just fastening his seatbelt when the taxi hit a bump in the road causing him to bang his head on the roof. They sped out of a small side street onto a main road and dropped back into the flow of traffic, two cars behind the black saloon.

Francois kept turning around to talk to the two boys. On one occasion, he mounted a kerb, narrowly missing an old woman struggling with a heavy shopping bag. Undeterred, the man insisted on talking to them at every opportunity.

"Football?" he asked. "I am fan of Blackburn United." He smiled, showing his nicotine-stained teeth.

"Rovers," corrected Holly, who was now safely fastened into his seatbelt.

"Yes, Rover, very good English car, but not as good as Citroën," replied Francois, tapping the centre console. BT's head hurt from Francois' continuous stream of meaningless conversation, helping him realise Martin often talked a lot of sense after all.

"Look out!" shouted BT in alarm. The traffic lights had just turned red. A car braked in front of the taxi. With lightning reflexes, Francois turned the wheel. BT braced himself as the taxi smacked into the kerb, missing the traffic light pole by inches. Francois steered the taxi away from collision with a shop window, but only to end up heading straight towards a fruit and vegetable stall.

Holly squeezed his eyes shut.

BANG!

Strangely enough, the car was still moving. Turning around, Holly slowly opened his eyes and peered out of the rear window in time to see apples, grapefruits, and one large melon rolling across the road.

"Where have they gone?" BT asked the driver. A fear of losing the gangsters left a hollow sensation in the pit of his stomach. BT knew Jack would never have lost sight of them. He could hear Jack's voice now, reminding them how he had caught Elizabeth Coldaire red-handed with the treasure and how BT had let the rest of the team down.

Suddenly, Francois brought the car to a screeching halt. Letting out a dull groan, BT slammed into the back of Francois' seat.

"We are here..." whooped Francois, nodding across the road. BT could not see the car anywhere. Then he spotted the car parked halfway down a narrow alley. "But you don't want to be alone in these parts, my adventurous friends. Very dangerous!"

"We've got protection," smiled Holly, pointing towards BT.

"Ah!" nodded Francois. "You really are the young Bonds. Well, if you know what you're doing, that'll errr..." Francois paused as he looked at his metre, "special price to you of only twelve-euros and–" Before Francois could finish his sentence BT slapped a twenty euro note in his open palm and jumped out of the car. "But what about your change?" Francois called after the departing boys. "Pah! Crazy English!" Francois muttered as he drove off.

BT and Holly ran across the road before stooping behind a parked car. They were glad to be away from Francois and his crazy driving. Using the refracto-glasses once again, BT could see over the top of the car bonnet. Safe from fear of being spotted, he watched as the two men got out of their car. After stopping for a brief conversation, the men disappeared into the building directly opposite the parked car.

For a moment, the boys sat in silence. The chase had been exhilarating, but this was the real deal. This was no longer a childish game. They turned to look at one another and without a word slowly climbed to their feet. The decision had been made. They were going to continue.

Entering the narrow side street, BT was sure he saw someone move up ahead. He blinked and looked again, but there was no one there. His mind must be playing tricks. An uneasy feeling washed over him.

They slowly approached the stationary car with the blacked-out windows. As they got closer, no one needed to tell them where the two men had gone. Coming from the only building looking like it wasn't about to fall down, the beat of music playing loud could be heard half-way down the street. BT then noticed two large men standing either side of a door. Unless he was a monkey's uncle, they were definitely bouncers.

"What now?" whispered Holly as they both ducked into a nearby doorway.

In his mind, Holly was hoping BT's response would be: "Okay...we've gone as far as we can. It's too dangerous and I'm starving. Let's get back to the hotel in time for tea. I remember hearing it was shepherd's pie and chips." A vision of being back at the hotel and tucking into his favourite meal evaporated as soon as BT spoke. "I have a plan...just follow my lead." BT turned and walked towards the two security men. "Ohhh..." he groaned, whilst holding his crotch. "Excuse me, mister. Please can we use the bathroom? We desperately need to pee."

Holly was impressed with BT's plan. Jumping out into the open he began following BT's lead. "Oh, yes sir, we've been drinking fizzy pop all afternoon and need to go to the bathroom desperately," said Holly, jumping up and down on the spot.

The men looked at each other with blank expressions.

"Pleassse?" pleaded BT desperately to the two huge security men. Their shoulders alone were wider than a truck. If the plan failed, the boys could end up flatter than pancakes. As if BT had just used some Jedi mind trick, the two bodyguards stepped aside and indicated they were alright to enter.

"Did you see that?" said Holly, shocked that they had actually managed to get inside. "I didn't think your plan would actually work."

"I know," laughed BT, "neither did I."

"What? You mean you came up with an idea you figured was never going to work? I mean, did you see the size of those guys? I was terrified. It felt like we were little hobbits walking past two orcs."

"My precious," laughed BT as he pulled his one and only spy-fly out of his pocket and began stroking it.

"Come on, Mr. Frodo," coaxed Holly. "We need to act serious."

"Have you been eating all our bread, Sam?" asked BT.

"Why you know I have, Mr. Frodo, sir. It wouldn't be right to let you have any at all. My need for fuel stimulation is greater than yours," laughed Holly.

"Stop it, my stomach hurts," said BT, leaning on a wall for support while trying to control his hysterics.

Just then, a giant of a man walked past, knocking BT to the ground. Holly wanted to shout, "Be careful you brutish oaf!" The man turned and stared at Holly. On this occasion, Holly backed off, deciding not to push the issue any further.

BT lifted himself up off the carpet and back onto his feet. "Where's my fly?" he asked in panic, frantically scanning the floor. Dropping to his knees BT urgently started brushing the carpet with his palms. "Quick mate, I've lost my fly. That big ape knocked it out of my hands. You've gotta help me find it."

"Don't move," said Holly.

"OUCH!" howled BT.

"Sorry," replied Holly. "At least I found your spy-fly. It was caught in your hair."

"I know that now, don't I..." whined BT, "but there was no need to pull all my hair out was there?" BT picked himself up off the floor for a second time before setting off down the corridor.

The two boys pushed open a door to find a dimly lit room so full of cigarette smoke it felt more like standing in early morning fog. They were in a nightclub, which seemed strange considering it was early in the evening.

"Over there!" Holly nudged his friend.

BT immediately saw the two men seated in a booth drinking a couple of beers. They were alone.

"Right," said BT, "I'm gonna send my spy-fly over onto his jacket and then we're in business."

"Hold on..." cautioned Holly. "You're tellin' me that's your big plan? Are you insane? We'll never get close enough. This is suicide," choked Holly, his throat burning from the excessive amount of smoke in the room. It felt as though his wind pipe was closing up.

"Just watch," smiled BT, cool as ice. He placed his spy-fly on his open palm and with his other hand, pressed a button on his mobile phone. Holly watched in astonishment as the spy-fly's wings flickered into life. With a tiny buzz, it lifted off and hovered in the air. "See...you dared to doubt moi?" grinned BT.

Stunned into silence, Holly gawked as BT took full control of his mobile phone and began to operate the buttons as though he was holding a remote control. The spy-fly zoomed into life and started buzzing its way across the room undetected. Holly watched in a trance as the tiny electronic spying device flew towards the two Russian mobsters. It looked like fun. Holly wanted to try. Without stopping to think, he grabbed the controls from BT.

"Careful," snapped BT, flashing Holly a look of disdain. "Now look what you've made me—"

"Yeah, well I only wanted a quick go," said Holly, trying to defend his behaviour before BT could complain any further.

"Lucky for you, it landed on the lapel of his coat. So no harm done I suppose. Just don't snatch at it next time."

"I didn't snatch," argued Holly.

"For your information," BT pointed out, "this is an expensive piece of technical equipment. It takes a lot of practice to handle this device."

"So what now?" asked Holly, trying to keep up with BT's ever-evolving plan of action.

"We go back to the hotel, tune into this audio app on my phone and we have instant access to every plan or move they... Oh no!" BT interrupted himself.

"What, what's wrong?" asked Holly anxiously.

"The guy's accidently knocked my spy-fly off onto the floor." Just then BT put his hand over his mouth to prevent a loud gasp. "Phew! He just missed stepping on it."

"What did I miss? What's happening?" asked Holly jumping up and down trying to see what was happening.

"It landed under their table. We're going to have to get it back somehow," said BT, scratching his head purposefully, almost as if he was hatching another harebrained scheme. Holly feared the worst. "Yes, that's it..." said BT proudly. "We can go back to the fancy dress shop and hire a dog outfit. Then you can pretend to be sniffing around under the table, pick up the fly, and attach it to—"

"No chance…I'm not being a dog," said Holly who stopped listening to BT's idea as soon as he heard the words, 'Fancy dress shop.'

"Well, you're the one who messed it up trying to grab the remote," BT pointed out.

"No I didn't and—" argued Holly.

"Ha-ha!" laughed BT. "I'm just messing with you… relax."

"It's a bit difficult to relax when you are in a gangster's lair and the plan's gone wrong and any minute—"

"What're you two doing here?" boomed a loud voice.

They both looked up. A very tall man with a shaved head, wearing a black tee shirt and a dark suit, towered over them. He was built like an ox. It was impossible to determine where the man's head finished and his neck started. Unusually for Holly, he could not think of anything to say. His mind had gone completely blank. It was almost like his built in self-defence mechanism had caused his eyes to shut and his knees to shake. Thankfully, BT was made from sterner stuff.

"We're trying to find the bathroom and got lost…" he whined. The man stared at them without even blinking. "If we don't find it quick, my friend's not going to be able to control himself any longer and pee all over the carpet. If you don't stand back, it will probably end up dribbling over your shiny shoes, too."

Holly opened his eyes in time to see the man take a

step backwards. "It's that door over there, and you better make it quick. You're not supposed to be in here." BT grabbed Holly by the arm, pulling him towards the purple door the man had just pointed to. As they crossed the room, every head turned and stared, making Holly feel like he must be covered in luminous paint.

As they entered the toilet, a rancid smell scorched Holly's nostrils. BT dropped to his hands and knees, checking under the cubicle doors, ensuring they were alone. "Hurry up, mate..." urged Holly. "I can't stand it in here. It smells as if something died a month ago!"

BT quickly explained his plan to recover the spy-fly. Holly was convinced their mission would not only fail but they would end up in the biggest pickle imaginable.

They both approached the table where the two Russians were sitting. Without warning, Holly pushed BT.

"Watch who you're pushing, mate..." BT pushed his hand against Holly's chest, shoving him backwards.

"Don't tell me to watch it," Holly retaliated, shoulder barging BT.

"I-said-don't-do-that," snapped BT.

"I-will-do-what-I-like," Holly snapped back, shoving BT so hard he went sprawling onto the floor with a bang.

"Now look what you've gone and done," BT cried out shuffling around on the floor. "You've gone and lost my contact lens." He proceeded to sweep his hands over surface of the floor underneath the table where the two

Russians sat, looking baffled.

"What do you think you're doing?" said one of the gangsters, the one with a strong American accent.

This was the part where Holly knew he was supposed to do something, only he had forgotten. The man stood up and began talking louder, straight at Holly. Any second, the man would surely lose his temper because Holly could not reply. Then a little voice in his head told him to dance. Without questioning the command, Holly slowly began to shuffle his feet.

The craziest thing imaginable began to happen, it actually worked.

"Look Vladimir! It's a dancing monkey," said the man, slowly sitting back down with a chuckle.

"I've found it!" a small cry of jubilation echoed out from underneath the table. BT emerged and gave Holly a sly wink as he slipped the bug into the man's jacket pocket. Operation spy-fly was a success.

All that was left to do was to get out of the place, alive!

Chapter Nineteen

Jack, Jules, and Martin were trapped, waist-deep in sewage water, the smell bringing tears to Jack's eyes. If suffering from hyperthermia did not kill them, the terrible stench definitely would.

"Hello!" shouted Martin, hoping to attract someone's help to undo his mess. "Is there anyone thereee?" His question bounced all around the inside of the copper drum, repeating itself over and over. "Helloooo!" called Martin again, momentarily distracted from their plight, enjoying the sound of his voice echoing.

"Pack it in, will ya?" barked Jack, gloomily.

"What if no one ever finds us?" asked Jules. She was right. Although Jack did not want to admit it, there was a distinct possibility they may never be found.

"Don't be daft, sis..." soothed Martin, "Of course, someone will find us, even if it's in the morning when the-hey come to wo-wo-wo-rk." Martin's teeth were beginning to chatter from the cold water.

"But you're forgetting something...this place is derelict. There might not be anyone around for days, possibly weeks," reminded Jules, annoyed. "And this stupid stuff..." She had gotten herself caught up in reams of plastic mesh and was frantically trying to free herself.

"When you've finished splashing around like a drunken octopus, I've been looking everywhere for a way out. Apart from the hatch we fell through, the only other exit is that door up there, but it looks about thirty feet up," pointed Jack.

"Well what about a ladder or s-s-s-ome-th-th-ing," chattered Martin.

"Don't be so thick! We're in the bottom of a sewage tank. There ain't gonna be a ladder just lying around..." said an unimpressed Jules.

"Well som-som-someone better come up with a plan so-oo-oon," quivered Martin. "I'm fer-ree-eezing."

Martin was right. The gravity of their situation was quickly becoming evident. They needed a miracle. As far as Jack could see, they weren't just running out of options, there were no more options.

After realising Elizabeth Coldaire had led them into a trap, Jack had been trying to think of a reason why. What was her secret? How did George Martin fit into it? What was the significance of the key, the hooded figures and Rouen? What was the connection between them all? Now none of that mattered, the only thing Jack was interested in was getting out, and quick!

His mind drifted to thoughts of his mum and dad. An image of his mum lying in bed passed through his mind. He might never get the chance to tell her how much he cared.

"Wh-what was th-that?" chattered Martin.

"Oh please, will you give it a rest – just this once? I'm cold! Tired! Caught up in this stupid plastic mesh... and the smell is killing me. Won't you ever just grow up?" pleaded Jules, pulling the plastic coils from her arm.

"Ouch...something definitely bit me," yelped Martin, jumping around like a raving lunatic. "I'm being serious!"

"Martin, don't move! There's something moving in the water towards you. I can see its gleaming red eyes," said Jack in a serious tone. "I think it might be rats."

"Rats!" shrieked Martin. "I hate rats!"

"JACK! Is that you?" a voice shouted, echoing around the copper prison. "Are you down there?"

A light flashed. Jack looked up in surprise. Someone was there who knew his name, but he could not make out whom. Jack's first instinct was that Elizabeth Coldaire had returned. The voice certainly sounded female, but whoever it was sounded too young to have been the movie star. It almost sounded like... He shook his head. He knew it could not possibly be...

"Emma? Is that you?" quizzed Jules, still struggling to untangle herself from the last piece of plastic netting.

"What're you doing here?" shouted Jack. "You should be back at the hotel."

"Who cares about that? She can go and ger-get help!" Martin shouted at Jack before turning his attention to Emma. "Hurry up, Emma," he urged. "There's loads of rats down here... BIG ones, with radioactive eyes!"

"Don't worry," she promised. "I've got an idea!" The light disappeared.

"Where's she gone?" asked Jack, confused.

"Why can't she hurry up?" groaned Martin, constantly spinning around and checking there weren't any rats near him. Every so often, he would swipe at the water with a stick he had found floating amongst the debris, hoping to keep the unwanted vermin at arm's length.

Jack could hear noises from above. He knew Emma was up to something but could not work out what it was.

"I'm back," she called out. "I'm throwing down a rope for you." With a splash, a length of rope landed in the water next to Jules. "You'll need to grab it and hold on tight."

Jack hesitated. There was not a chance Emma would be able to pull all three of them to safety.

"Come on, Jack…" said Jules, already climbing the rope glad to be pulling herself free from the murky sewage.

"Wait for me," yelled Martin. "You're not leaving me down here with those things!" He swam the final meter in record time, grabbing hold of the rope as fast as he could. Jack wanted to argue the stupidity of Emma's plan, but he also did not want to spend any more time amongst the rotting filth, freezing water, and hungry rats with the burning red eyes.

Grabbing hold of the rope, Jack tried to haul himself up only for his hands to slip. It was as though the rope was covered in grease. Suddenly, he could feel himself rising out of the ice cold water.

The rope had pulled Jack to within touching distance

of the exit. Jules was already clambering through the hole to safety with Martin right behind her.

Jack's hand slipped once again, jarring his shoulder. He was struggling to hold onto the greasy rope with the pain in his arm intensifying. His strength was failing. He was so cold he could not feel his fingers. Too tired! Just before everything went dark, a hand wrapped tightly around Jack's wrist, pulling him out of harm's way.

Opening his eyes Jack found the room spinning. "J-a-c-k, are-you-alright?" Martin's voice bore into his subconscious.

"I'm fine," replied Jack, still lying on his back.

Two pairs of hands roughly pulled him to his feet. Jack felt shaky. His jeans clung tightly to his legs as he staggered away from the toxic smell.

The three friends, soaking wet and freezing cold, along with Emma, climbed down a short flight of steps and sat down on crates that were scattered everywhere. They were in some sort of workshop lit by a couple of rusty industrial lights fastened to the walls. The flickering lights emitted an orange glow. A square generator clunked noisily in the background and Jack could see how Emma had been able to rescue them from the sewage pit. The rope coiling around its drum reminded Jack of his dad's garden hose pipe he used for his vegetable patch – Roger's pride and joy.

"Brrr, it's fer-ree-eezing," chattered Martin as he stood shivering, dripping wet from head to toe. "H-how did you know where to find us?"

"I've been following you," said Emma proudly, wiping the sweat from her brow. Her face shone brighter than the lights on the wall.

"What...you mean ever since we left the hotel?" asked Jules sounding impressed before changing her tone to one of disapproval. "You shouldn't have been running around the city on your own like that," she admonished. "It's not safe!"

"What were you thinking...? You're supposed to be looking after my mum!" shouted Jack.

"I'm sorry," said Emma, slowly bowing her head and twirling her hair between her fingers.

"Hodge-podge! You were ace and I'm glad you did," praised Martin, leaning over and slapping her on the back.

"Jack, don't be so mean. If it wasn't for Emma, you'd be stuck down there. Then who knows when you'd see your mum – or anyone else," snapped Jules.

"Erm, I suppose so," acknowledged Jack before adding a lame, "Thank you."

"Oh my poor Lola," Jules interrupted.

"Never mind about Lola, if my mum finds out I'm not there, my life won't be worth living. Besides, I have to get out of these filthy, wet, stinking clothes," stated Jack, annoyed at everything. Their whole day had been a complete waste of time. They were no nearer to figuring out the key's secret. Elizabeth Coldaire had given them the slip. Emma had left his mum – who had a fever – all alone. And all Jules was bothered about was her precious rabbit.

"Your mum was fast asleep and Lola's safe," replied Emma, pulling the one-eyed rabbit out of a cardboard box on top of a workbench. Lola was happily munching on a crisp lettuce leaf.

"Lola! You're safe!" cried Jules excitedly. She rushed over and began rubbing her nose in the rabbit's fur. "Have you missed me?" she cooed.

Jack sighed.

"Ah, but you can't, Jack," said Martin, his reaction to Jack's predicament a little slow.

"I can't what?" asked Jack, confused.

"You can't get changed out of your wet, smelly clothes. You left all your clothes back on the minibus. Remember?" said Martin cheerily.

Now Jack was utterly depressed.

Chapter Twenty

Tripping over their own feet, BT and Holly retreated towards the exit, desperate to get away. Holly could feel his eyes stinging from the excessive smoke in the room. In a few seconds, they would be outside, out in the fresh air where they would be able to breathe properly again. They entered the long, carpeted corridor connecting the seedy room to the exit. Safety was only a few feet away.

"Stop!" A man with a Russian accent shouted. BT's heart sank.

The game was up. "Keep moving," whispered BT, quickening his pace hoping they would make it to the exit in time.

"You boys, stop!" The Russian repeated, only louder this time.

They were almost at the door. One more step and BT would be able to grab the door. Just as he reached for the handle, the door swung open, almost as though it had operated on its own accord. One of the two security men from outside, built like a brick wall, barred their escape to safety. There was no way out.

A large paw of a hand grabbed BT's shoulder.

"My friend... Why you run? You drop this..." a deep voice asked. BT turned slowly around to see the man offering him what appeared to be his mobile phone – except, it could not possibly be. BT's phone was tucked safely in his pocket. He patted his jeans. Oh, no! It wasn't there! His hand shot to check his jacket pocket. "You drop this under table while crawling on the floor like little puppy," explained the Russian. The man's head dropped backwards as he let out a huge roar of laughter.

Grateful, BT snatched his phone out of the man's huge hand. His fingers were as big as Cumberland sausages.

The evening spring air was a welcome sensation on BT's overheated skin as he stepped outside. He had often dreamt about moments like that, of being a secret child agent for the government and taking on the world's toughest criminals. But, if the job offer ever presented itself, especially after what he had just been through, he would run a mile.

Once safe and sound back in their hotel room, they would be able to laugh about the whole escapade. No doubt, the story would evolve into a full epic espionage novel where he, with the help (but only a very tiny bit) from his trusted sidekick, Holly, entered the den of the biggest, most dangerous criminals in the world and, singlehandedly, made them regret they had ever crossed his path. He was a super-sleuth!

***

Walking back to the hotel, Jack felt fed-up. He smelled worse than rotten fish. People either gave him and his friends a wide berth on the pavement or looked at them with odd expressions. Even Emma walked two feet behind them complaining about the foul pong. An elderly woman wearing a flowery headscarf, made a tut-tut sound as she walked by them. To make things worse, every time Jack placed a foot down on the pavement, it would let out a great, sloppy, squish.

As they rounded the final corner, a man in a long robe crossed the street, heading straight towards them. Jack was paranoid. Anybody in a long robe or wearing a hood was definitely not to be trusted. Jack jumped into the nearest opening, a tiny alleyway between two buildings.

"What you doing you wet fish?" asked Martin, unaware of any potential danger.

"Quick!" hissed Jack, gesturing for them to follow. It was a tight squeeze. Last to enter the narrow alleyway was Emma, carrying Lola.

Before Jack had a chance to explain why they were squashed like sardines, the hooded man appeared at the entrance. There was nowhere else to go.

The man stepped closer and grabbed Emma. She tried to scream, but the man roughly placed his hand over her mouth. "Give me the key!" he demanded.

Jack did not know what do, but this was the very reason he did not want Emma with them. He tried lamely to think of an escape plan, but they were trapped. There was nothing he could do.

"Lola!" screamed Jules as the one-eyed rabbit leapt from Emma's grasp.

Lola bit the man on his ankle, making him shriek like a little girl. Emma elbowed the man in his ribs. While the man was hopping on one foot and off balance, Emma turned around quickly and pushed him. The man crashed like a tree that had just been chopped by a lumberjack. Without waiting for the others, Emma scooped Lola safely into her arms and clambered over the fallen man. Making his escape, Jack jumped over the man who let out a dull groan.

Jack's squelchy trainers pounded the pavement. They were only a few yards from the hotel. He kept checking over his shoulder to make sure they were not being followed.

Soaking wet, freezing cold and tired – not to mention hungry – Jack could happily have eaten a hundred cardboard-tasting croissants. He made it back to the hotel just ahead of his friends. Jack could not wait to get out of his filthy wet clothes. He was looking forward to a nice hot shower, even if the shower did have a mind of its own, randomly turning itself to freezing half way through washing his hair. That is when he decided to get to their hotel room first, so he would definitely get first dibs on the bathroom.

Still shaken by their encounter with the hooded man, Jack was halfway across the foyer when the main doors behind him swung open. In came Martin, followed by Jules, and then finally, Emma appeared with Lola safely tucked in her arms. Drat! He would not have enough time to get into the lift and close the doors before they breached the gap. If he wanted to be the first to the shower he would just have to make sure he shoved them out of the way when they exited the lift.

Suddenly, a voice shattered his plans. Any plotting of his dash to the bathroom was wiped from memory.

"Not to worry, then," spoke a distinctive voice. "If you do get any information on the matter, please get in touch. Here's my number."

Turning with dread towards the reception desk, Jack froze. Standing there, with his back to them, wearing his usual pinstripe suit, his hair looking like it had been slicked back with a whole tub of axle grease, was Inspector David Tyrrell.

Chapter Twenty One

An avalanche of questions began cascading into Jack's head: *Why ... what ... how?*

"Quick! Over here..." ordered Jules. Jack stood and gawked at Jules diving behind an enormous terracotta pot. It was astonishing how Jack had failed to notice the giant, dark green plant before he thought, as he dove for cover behind it. Fortunately, the large leafy plant was substantial enough to conceal all four children as they squatted unceremoniously behind it.

Peering through the plants giant size leaves like a tribal native of the Amazon rain forest, Jack watched David Tyrrell say his good-byes before walking towards the exit. As the Police Inspector was about to step through the hotel door, he paused. Jack held his breath. Like frozen statues, they kept as still as they could. Oddly, David Tyrrell seemed to be sniffing the air. Jack realised how badly he and his friends smelled. It was a complete giveaway!

"Phew, what a pong!" complained Tyrell, wrinkling his nose. The game was surely up. "I suggest you get your drains checked out. It's not good for a respectable business." At that, he turned and headed through the hotel doors that led into the street outside.

They waited until David Tyrrell was long gone before emerging from their leafy hideout. The thought of getting to the shower first no longer seemed important. "What on earth?" he simply said, finding it difficult to comprehend why the Police Inspector had travelled all the way from Barnoldswick to arrive in Rouen.

"Blimey!" breathed Martin, just as surprised. "What's *he* doing here?"

"I knew there was something dodgy about him all along," said Jack, trying to stop his soaking jeans from sticking to his legs. Nothing made any sense.

"Well, there's no point standing here in our wet clothes discussing it. We might as well get back to our room and get changed," said Jules.

"Bagsy the shower first, then," said Martin, sprinting towards the lift.

"Hey, you can't..." complained Jack. "I was back at the hotel first."

"Yeah," countered Martin, "but you didn't bagsy the shower first, did you?"

"No, I didn't need t–"

"Well, there you go then. I bagsied it and I've got Jules and Emma as witnesses," said Martin triumphantly. Soaked to the bone and extremely tired, Martin still found enough energy to lift his shoulders and walk proudly into the lift as if he had just won a gold medal.

***

"Right then, all I need to do is press this button and voila...we should be in business," explained BT, getting comfortable on one of the double beds in their hotel bedroom.

"Here...let me have a look then," said Holly, peering over his friends shoulders to get a better view.

Not happy with just watching, Holly attempted to snatch the phone to have a go himself. BT was still busy fending off Holly when it chimed into life. After a short whine, like the sound of radio interference, someone speaking in English with a strong Russian accent could distinctly be heard: "...*That's what I was saying, Michael.*"

"*Do you think they know where it is?*" followed the response.

"*That's what George reckons. He said–*" BT didn't hear what was next. Their hotel room door burst open and in tumbled Martin and Jack, wrestling each other to the ground. "I bagsied..." panted Martin.

Jules calmly stepped over the writhing mass and entered the bathroom, locking the door behind her.

A sharp trill emitted from BT's phone, followed by silence. "Of all the rotten luck..." he moaned.

"Why? What's up? Is your battery dead?" asked Holly. Martin and Jack were still grappling with each other on the floor. Suddenly, Jack managed to pry himself away from Martin's grasp. Quick as a flash, he leapt to his feet and ran to the bathroom.

SMACK!

He collapsed in a heap rubbing his forehead.

"Too late," said Emma smiling at Jack crashing into the locked door. "Jules has already beaten you to it."

"And what's that awful smell?" asked BT, instantly pinching his nose.

"It's a long story," groaned Martin, getting up off his hands and knees, looking more dishevelled than a dozen drowned rats. "What're you two up to? Did you manage to tail the two crooks?"

"We did..." said BT, "but the stupid thing's stop working. It's like something's causing interference." Hoping to get a better reception, BT began wandering around the room holding his phone in the air.

"What? You mean we went through all that danger and now it's not even working?" moaned Holly, at the same jumping off the bed.

It soon became like a tag boxing match. In the blue corner, Jack and Martin, slugging it out against Holly and BT in the red corner, to claim bragging rights of the most adventurous and exciting afternoon. Although it became apparent that both parties equally had action-packed afternoons, neither side wanted to admit defeat. Eventually, both camps went back to their corners to evaluate the judge's scores. In this case, the judge's panel was made up of Emma and Jules' one eyed rabbit, Lola.

Smelling like roses, Jules emerged from the bathroom. One white bath towel was wrapped around her body and another circled her head like a turban. It was the rematch the boys had been waiting for. A wall of chatter erupted while everyone tried to get their two cent's worth in. Jack decided, while Martin was busy exaggerating their lame pursuit of Elizabeth Coldaire, he would make a dash for the shower. Just as he was about to make his move, a voice called his name. It was his mum in the next room.

His mum began asking Jack lots of questions about his day ... what had he been up to ... where had he been? At least he did not get into any more trouble. Just when he thought she had finished talking, she asked if he would be a love and make her a cup of tea. Huffing and puffing, he wandered over to the side table where the small hotel kettle, cups and saucers and a wicker basket full of biscuits were housed. All the biscuits in the kids' room had mysteriously vanished during the night.

Finally, Jack escaped his mum's attention only to discover that Martin had claimed the bathroom. Holly and BT were dancing around the room, whooping jubilantly, having won the bragging rights for the best adventure. Jack demanded a rematch on the premise that they had only won by default.

"Well, it's not our fault," stated Holly, peering down his nose at Jack. "You and Martin weren't here."

"I'd like to see how you would have survived, stuck in a vat full of water, especially as BT's got a water phobia."

"Aha...but I wouldn't have gotten wet," BT pointed out, pulling an ordinary looking aerosol can out of his backpack and waving his latest invention around triumphantly. The argument started all over again.

By the time the bathroom was free all the hot water had been used. There was no way Jack could go to bed smelling so bad. The only way of getting any hot water was by boiling it in the tiny hotel kettle. It held the equivalent of three dessert spoonfuls of water and not a drop more. It took Jack a full half-hour just to fill the sink.

That night, Jack lay awake in bed, convinced that his holiday was jinxed.

The Keep

Chapter Twenty Two

Life had not been kind to Jack since his arrival in France. Hopefully, all his troubles were behind him. He awoke with a huge smile on his face. That morning they were off to Rouen Cathedral to investigate the key's secret.

The fact he had no clean clothes to wear did not dampen Jack's spirits. Thankfully, Martin had a spare pair of jeans. Holly had plenty of tops, although most of his clothes were slightly too big for Jack. Somehow, he managed to find one pale blue polo shirt that fit. It was one thing borrowing Holly's top and Martin's jeans, but another matter entirely with other items he really needed. There was no way in the world he was going to borrow anyone else's underwear.

The evening before, after Jack washed the majority of the foul odour from his body, he washed his socks and underpants, using a half bottle of Jules' shampoo and hung them out to dry. It was a good thing his dad was not around. Roger Hunter would have gone ballistic at finding Jack's washing hung out to dry all over the apartment's bathroom.

Jack had found out that his dad finally found a place to charge his phone and was able to speak to his mum. Roger Hunter blamed it on the French having different electricity sockets rather than admitting he had forgotten to bring a European plug adaptor. His dad and Grandad were both safe and would be arriving the following day, in time to take them to Disneyland for the last few days of their holiday.

Out-voting Jack four to one, Emma had been allowed to go to the cathedral. Everyone thought she was shy. They never saw that she always made a beeline for Jack.

"I don't believe it. I must have been so stupid..." said Holly.

"Yep, I agree with that," laughed Martin, pulling on Emma's pigtails like they were a pair of reins, at the same time making silly horsey noises.

"It all makes sense now. I can't believe I didn't think of it earlier," said Holly, ignoring Martin's silly antics.

"Think of what?" asked Jack, intrigued.

"Well, we're in Rouen and on our way to Rouen Cathedral...Yeah...?"

"I guess that would make sense," said BT, scratching his head.

"What...don't you see?" Holly looked dumfounded that none of his friends understood the significance. "Rouen Cathedral is where King Richard the Lionheart is buried!"

"Is that Richard the First or Richard the Second?" chirped Martin.

"Shurrup, Martin," snapped Jules.

"What?" shrugged Martin, looking around to his mates for moral support. "I'm being serious."

"Richard the First," sighed Jack.

"Well, when I say *buried*, not all of him is buried there. His heart is buried in Rouen...his entrails were buried in Chalus–"

"What're entrails?" interrupted Martin.

"It's just a posh word for guts," said Jules, prodding her brother in his stomach.

"Urgh!" said Emma sticking her tongue out.

"And the rest of his body was buried in Fontevraud Abbey," finished Holly, proudly.

"But what's so amazing about that? *History should be kept a mystery* is what I say," laughed Martin, earning a high five from BT.

"Argh! Sometimes you're all so juvenile. You remember the three lions used by King Richard the Second on the coin that Jack's grandad gave him? The one connected to the treasure? Well, the symbol was his calling card to certain members of the Four Corners to reunite the Lionheart. The three lions represented King Richard being buried in three different places. Don't tell me, after all we went through last summer, that you've forgotten everything?" asked Holly in disbelief.

"Well, no, I remember the grave with all the skulls and that," said Martin, frantically trying to remember at least one piece of useful information.

"You're right. Don't you think this is all a little bit creepy?" said Jack in a hushed voice. "First of all, we had all that funny Four Corner business last year, and then we end up stumbling across not one, but two medieval keys that lead to some ancient treasure involving the same two Kings – again. And not only that, but we have David Tyrrell creeping around. It's spooky."

"I agree. The fact we're right here in this stupid place when we're supposed to be in Paris, and that key you found just happens to have a clue pointing to – let me guess! Ah, yes! – this town. It's way too big to be a coincidence," added BT.

The conversation continued with theories and counter theories as they all added their own opinion. In no time at all, they found themselves at the front of the cathedral.

"So what're we looking for exactly?" asked Emma, who was relatively new to the whole treasure hunting business.

"Something that sticks out as different," said Martin running up the stone steps leading to the entrance.

Jack took the old key out of his pocket in the hope that some flash of inspiration might magically point the way to the treasure. Nothing jumped out at him, so he passed the key to Jules who began to scour it carefully on both sides.

"And you're certain these numbers point to this exact location?" she asked, looking at Emma. Emma nodded her head in confirmation. "Well, if that's the case," said Jules, "then I suggest whatever we're supposed to be looking for is something to do with these other numbers that are inscribed around the key's handle in Roman numerals. One, two, three, two, six and a four."

"What exactly, do they mean? Is it like a date or time?" asked Jack, trying to look intelligent.

"Don't be daft! They wouldn't go around writing a secret clue and then think, '*Oh! Let's put the time on it as well,*'" huffed Holly.

"Well at least I'm trying to think of something...aren't I?" said Jack defensively. "What about you? Have you got any ideas then?"

"Look! We don't know what it is, but just keep your eyes open. The numbers could mean something important," calmed Jules.

"Okay then, I suggest that me, Martin, and Jules go this way and you three go that way," said Jack, trying to take control of the situation.

"But why does Emma have to come with us?" moaned Holly.

"Because... these are the same teams as yesterday, at least us three were, so you get Emma to make your team into three. Then, whoever finds the clue is the ultimate winner – seeing as yesterday was technically a draw," explained Jack.

"No! We won yesterday," hissed BT.

Before they could get into another argument about whose was the best team, Jules grabbed Jack and Martin by their collars, pulling them away from the boyish confrontation. Jack was not impressed. He still felt a little miffed that the others had claimed victory by default. He wanted to prove he was the best.

They set about their task, weaving their way through the crowded cathedral, tourists swarming everywhere like ants. This was the bit about clue finding and treasure hunting Jack disliked the most. He never knew what they were looking for, and when he did, someone else always seemed to find it first.

All the marble statues and stone archways in the cathedral looked the same. Looking at the height of the ceilings made Jack question why medieval buildings were so tall. From memory of history – which was not very much – he never recalled, not once, any reference to people in olden times being ten-feet-tall.

Jack was determined that his team would find the next clue. They looked everywhere; the ceilings, behind doors, down narrow passages, and even under the waste bins. Absolutely nothing! After searching the cathedral from top to bottom for the umpteenth time and finding nothing, they all decided to call it a day. Hungry and tired, they just wanted to be back at the hotel.

They dragged themselves back to the hotel in low spirits. Anyone would have thought Jules' rabbit had died from the way they moped along in silence. In a way, Jack half wished Lola had died, just to get the old Jules back. She was more interested in her rabbit than figuring out the key's secret. He watched as she strolled ahead with Lola tucked under her arm, every so often petting the rabbit on its head. Jack was sure if the rabbit could talk, the first words Lola would say would be, *Stop patting my head.* In his opinion, continuous head-patting was likely to give the poor rabbit brain damage.

Jack gazed ahead thinking how silly the pair looked. He froze, struck with fear at what he saw in front of them.

"Jules!" shouted BT suddenly.

Snapping into action, Jack rushed forward, grabbing Jules by the wrist and yanking her backwards. "Ouch!" she complained, trying to pull her arm free.

Holly and Emma were already running into a conveniently located side street with Martin right behind them. Realising something was wrong Jules glanced back over her shoulder. She immediately wished she hadn't. Three individuals, their faces hidden by hoods, were running towards them. "Hurry!" urged Jack.

Jack and BT ran along the street. Jules was right behind them, Lola tucked safely under her arm. The moment Jack heard the heavy footsteps of their three pursuers, any thought of over-reacting was quickly dispelled.

Without a clue where they were heading, Jack turned left in the same direction as Martin, Holly, and Emma had gone seconds earlier. Instead of seeing their friends just ahead of them, Jack, BT and Jules came face to face with a brick wall.

"It's a dead end!" cried Jules. Looking across the street, Jack's attention was drawn to a gate half concealed between two bushes swinging back and forth.

Without deliberation, Jack pushed open the gate.

They were now in someone's back garden, a stereotypical country garden with flowerbeds full of rose bushes and yellow Daffodils. "Over here..." shouted Holly beyond the vegetable patch. He then began lifting Emma over a tall wall.

As they ran down a path made from crazy-paving an unhappy looking woman appeared waving a walking stick in the air. "Sorry!" Jack apologised, decimating her prize cauliflowers before leaping over the garden wall.

At the other side of the wall, Jack nearly landed on top of Martin who lay crumpled in a heap on the ground.

"What're you doing down there, you clown?" asked Jack.

"I think I've twisted my ankle," wailed Martin, clutching his foot.

"We haven't got time for that," said Jack, yanking Martin mercilessly to his feet.

With Martin's arm draped around Jack's neck for support, they started running along a path by the side of the river. Disaster struck. A building backed right onto the riverbank. With the high wall on their left, the river to their right and the building in front of them, they were trapped!

Emma was only eight. Martin was an invalid. The hooded figures would soon be upon them. And Jack knew it was entirely his fault. They wanted the key.

Jack had a sudden brainwave. He was the fastest runner. If he could run back along the riverbank before the three thugs climbed over the garden wall, he might be able to lure them away from his friends. Then, they could make it to safety and alert the police.

Before Jack was able to announce his great idea, BT beat him to it with an idea of his own. "Stand back, everyone..." he ordered, "and be prepared to be amazed," he announced coolly. He whipped out something from his jacket, like a detective would produce a gun. "Ta-dah!" he herald, waving an aerosol can proudly.

"A tin of paint?" mocked Martin. "What good is that? Are you going to colour them to death?" he sneered.

"Ye of little faith," BT said airily. He fixed them with a look of disappointment before straightening his jacket collars and squaring his shoulders in preparation. "This is my newest invention – aeroSOLID!"

"Aerosol-id?" queried Martin. The look on his face was halfway between complete shock and mirth.

"It works on the principal of expanding cavity foam and–"

"There they are!" shouted a man, cutting BT's technical explanation short.

BT hurriedly gave the can a shake. The little piece of plastic inside rattled loudly. "Can't you hurry up?" begged Emma, an obvious tremble in her voice. Flipping the lid, BT crouched down and pointed the nozzle at the water. Flabbergasted, Jack leaned in closer. A quiet 'pssst' noise emitted from the nozzle. Nothing happened.

"Is that it?" howled Martin.

"We're done for!" groaned Jack.

Suddenly, a brown foamy substance that resembled silly string fired out from the end of the nozzle. As soon as it came into contact with the water it began to expand, rapidly.

"Hurry up!" urged Holly as the three people chasing them closed in.

"There...that should do it," announced BT.

Within seconds, a solid foam raft big enough to carry all six of them sat at the water's edge. Without wasting any time BT jumped aboard. "Quick, Emma," he said, "grab my hand."

The sound of crunching gravel caused Jack to look over his shoulder. The three hooded figures were nearly upon them. Making sure everyone else was safely aboard first Jack pushed the raft as hard as he could before jumping.

Splash!

Landing in the freezing cold water, Jack grabbed hold of the foam raft propelling it away from the embankment – and from their pursuers. Half way across the river, Holly and Martin hauled Jack on board. His friends were now frantically using their hands like oars, steering themselves across to the other side of the river.

"I-I'm s-s-s-soaked through...a-again," shivered Jack, now safely in the middle of the do-it-yourself vessel. Even Lola seemed happy as she lay curled up in a ball on Jules' lap. "Th-th-that's t-t-twice in t-t-t-two d-d-days." Jack's teeth chattered from his second cold swim of the week.

"Why do you think I invented aeroSOLID?" said BT with a smile. "You know I hate water. There was no way I was going to end up getting wet again. Not after last time when I nearly drowned."

The raft soon approached the opposite side of the river. BT was the first to jump onto dry land. Holly and Jules grabbed hold of Emma's hands swinging her to safety.

"Last one off is a loon," said Martin, racing Jack to get off. Eager to beat Martin, Jack lost his footing and fell backwards, creating a big splash.

Feeling miserable, Jack pushed all offers of help aside and stepped onto the embankment. "This is now officially the worst holiday, ever," Jack muttered under his breath.

"We need to hurry up," urged Jules. "It won't take long for them to find a way across, I'm sure I saw a bridge nearby," she announced.

Too late!!

On the nearby bridge Jack could hear shouting. Looking up he saw the silhouettes of three figures against the backdrop of the fading sun, already crossing the bridge towards them. Exasperated, wet, cold and frustrated, Jack's heart sank.

"Will they ever give up? What is it they want?" asked Holly.

"I think we should go this way," grimaced Martin, now limping badly.

They were never going to outrun the hooded gangsters and Jack was fresh out of ideas.

Suddenly, they heard the sound of tires screeching. They could see flashing headlights as a car sped towards them. They were trapped!

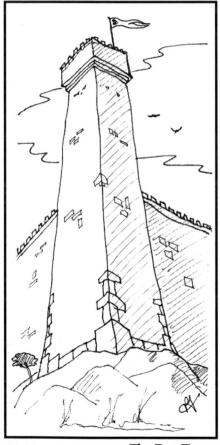

The East Tower

Chapter Twenty Three

Slamming on its brakes at the final moment, the speeding car screeched to a halt, inches from where Jack and his friends stood, blocking their escape route. There was nowhere to run. Jack watched in horror as the driver's door swung open and a man got out. It was all over.

Puzzlement followed as Jack soon recognised the portly man dressed in a suit. It was Roger Gante M.I.

"Quick... Get in!" ordered the man from Interpol. For a moment Jack could not move. His brain refused to send a message to his feet. "Hurry up," urged Roger in a frantic voice. There was no time for questions. Holly hastily climbed into the front seat forcing Jack and the others into the back seat. Peering out of the back window, Jack gladly watched the three creeps fading into the distance.

The journey back to the hotel was not the smoothest of car rides. Even the journey in the sickly yellow minibus had been better. Squashed in the back seat was worse than being a sardine. Martin accidently caught Jack in the face with an elbow as he wriggled to get comfortable. Before Jack could snap at him to watch what he was doing, Lola bounced onto his lap. Thankfully, Roger knew where they were staying and got them back safely in super-quick time.

"What intangible mess have you kids gone and gotten

yourselves caught up in, now?" asked a disgruntled Roger Gante as he brought the car to an abrupt halt right in front of the hotel doors. "I'm not sure who they were, but I will ensure that you are kept under protective surveillance at all times. If those creeps show their ugly faces around your hotel, they'll be dealt with."

"Thank you, sir," the boys all replied in unison.

"He's not that bad," said BT, wandering across the hotel foyer.

"He's saved us, again," added Martin, trying to pinch Lola without Jules noticing, just to see if the rabbit was still awake.

"But did anyone notice the markings on the stones by the river's edge?" asked Jules. "They had the symbol of the Four Corners etched into them. I'm sure of it."

"That's what I thought as well," agreed Holly.

"I'm tired," complained Emma tugging on her brother's arm.

"Look at that," gasped Jules, as if she had seen something really exciting, like six free VIP movie passes. "The date!" For some reason, Jules was staring at the reception desk.

Jack was gobsmacked. They had just endured a near-death experience, narrowly escaping the clutches of three dangerous, unidentified criminals, not to mention Jack's unfortunate double-soaking and all Jules could do was point to a digital clock that also displayed the day and month.

"Are you insane?" asked Jack, pointing his finger towards his head and moving it around, indicating he thought she had finally gone cuckoo.

"It's 19:37..." said Jules excitedly, as though it was both important and interesting. "On the fifth of the fourth," she added.

"I think she's lost her marbles. It must be all that time she spends talking to her rabbit," said Martin, shaking his head as he walked away from her, heading towards the elevator.

"Come on!" said Jules excitedly. Grabbing Jack by the hand and following Martin's lead she rushed towards the lift just as the door opened. Completely exhausted and without a clue as to what she was talking about, curiosity allowed Jack to be dragged along without a whimper.

Once they were back in their hotel room and safe from prying eyes in, convincing Jack to lend her the key Jules explained her theory. The six Roman numbers on the key they had not managed to decipher were, in fact, the time and date. Excitedly, she pointed out that 'one, two, three, two was actually twelve-thirty-two and 'six, four' was the sixth of April.

"But that's tomorrow," said Jack with astute awareness (although his blank face said otherwise.)

"I'm sure I know that date for a reason," said Holly, collapsing onto his bed, his face screwed up in concentration.

"Probably your grandmother's birthday," laughed

Martin, who was trying to shove the base of a table lamp up his tee shirt because it was the only item he could find that was the right length for scratching his back.

"At twelve-thirty-two tomorrow lunch time, I assume that some special event is going to happen," announced Jules, triumphantly.

"But this key is over six hundred years old, just like before, yeah?" inquired Martin with his usual carefree attitude while bouncing on the bed, deliberately causing Lola to jump awkwardly into the air. "So how could they predict all that long ago exactly what was going to happen tomorrow?"

Thinking about what Martin had just said, Jack watched as Emma dove to rescue Lola, scooping the rabbit safely into her arms. "Don't you think this is all very weird?" asked Jack to no one in particular. "It's like everything is falling perfectly into place ... finding the key ... arriving here by mistake ... and something happening tomorrow. It sounds too good to be true."

"I agree," said BT, joining in the conversation.

"But even if what you say is true, we still need to figure out what the numbers are actually pointing towards at Rouen Cathedral and–"

"And the way we found the key was fluky," Holly jumped in.

"Don't you mean the way *I* found the key?" asked Jack loudly.

"Jack, Jack? Is that you honey?" his mother called

weakly from the connecting room.

"Yes, Mum," answered Jack with a sigh. For a moment, he had forgotten all about his mum.

"Can you come here a minute?"

"Coming..." said Jack sullenly. Just before he reached the door, he noticed Holly with an object in his hand. Holly was holding a sugar-coated, jam doughnut. Jack could only stare as Holly licked his lips.

Jack was gutted. He was tired and his clothes were still damp, but more importantly, he was starving. Unlike Holly, he did not have a secret stash of doughnuts – he was clean out of food.

Chapter Twenty Four

A new day dawned, the sixth of April. Today Jack's dad and Grandad would finally be arriving in Rouen to join up with them. Since the discovery of Jules' rabbit, Jack dismissed the theory of sabotage. He figured Lola must have chewed through the engine wires, not cut by Russian gangsters like he first thought. No wonder Jules had been so sheepish. Although she had been mental for bringing the creature with her, on the plus side, it meant a *dad-free-holiday*, even if there had been no Disneyland.

Jack was relieved Jules wasn't bringing Lola to the cathedral, hoping instead it would help her remain focused. After the previous day's encounter with the three mysterious, hooded figures, they had unanimously voted, despite Emma's protests that both she and Lola stay behind. Jack's mum was on the mend, which was a major relief to him, even if he did not advertise the fact. He also realised how rubbish life would be without parents. Trying to fend for himself and sort his own meals over the last few days had not been easy. Having to remember what time breakfast was served or when to get ready for dinner was exhausting.

"We can't go out the front door," warned BT, tugging back on Martin's tee shirt.

"Why not?" asked Holly, trying to lick the last bit of syrup from his lips.

"Because...Roger Gante said he was putting his men outside the hotel for our protection. Remember? Well, don't you see? That means we can't go out the front door. Otherwise, they will try and stop us."

"That's right. They'll just say it's for our own protection," added Jack.

"More like they will say; *High-ho, he-ho, dischu lepoo sanap la peow*," laughed Martin, who realised by his friend's blank expressions they did not understand a word he was saying. "That's an impersonation of the police guys talking in French."

"I've an idea," said Jack, dismissing Martin's crummy accent. He ran back to the restaurant where they had just eaten breakfast – where Holly must have broken the record for eating the most syrup covered waffles in the hotel's history. After a few minutes, he re-emerged. "Quick! This way," beckoning his friends to follow him.

Mia, the young girl who worked part time at the front desk, showed them another way out of the hotel. The tradesmen's entrance meant they were able to leave undetected, under the very noses of the two plain-clothed policemen who were supposed to be watching out for them, sitting out front in their unmarked car.

"We're here," announced Holly proudly, as if he would get extra glory points for spotting the cathedral first. The time was five minutes to eleven. They had given themselves nearly two hours to find whatever it was they were looking for.

"But I don't get it," said Martin, who rarely understood most things. "What're we supposed to be looking for?"

"You'll know it when you see it," said Jules matter-of-factly. "According to the date and time on the key, something very important will be happening, but I just haven't figured out what."

"But how can I know it, if I don't know what IT is?" he protested. They entered a large room that contained the tomb of King Richard the Lionheart.

"If you'd spend more time looking and less time gobbing off, you might be of some use," preached Jules.

"I'm beginning to think we would have been better off letting Emma come and leaving Martin to look after your rabbit," added BT.

Martin immediately charged towards BT, hurling insults. There was a yellow plastic sign with an image depicting a slippery floor. Paying no attention to it, Martin tried to grab BT and make him pay for his slanderous comment. Comically, as if in slow motion, Martin's feet slipped from under him sending him flying into the air before slamming back down on his back.

"You're never going to believe this," said Holly while still chuckling at Martin sprawled on his back. "I've just remembered what's so important about today's date."

"We don't care that it's your grandma's birthday!" said Jack, more interested in watching Martin floundering on the floor, writhing through various stages of agony.

"No, you fool, not my grandma's birthday," exclaimed

Holly. "King Richard's!"

"What? Today is King Richard's birthday?" asked BT.

"Argh! Is no one listening? Today is the day that King Richard died. The sixth of April."

"Why would anyone want to celebrate the day he died?" asked Jack, puzzled.

"Er, mate? A helping hand would be appreciated," groaned Martin, still lying on the floor.

"Look at this plaque here," said Jules, completely ignoring Martin's pleas for help. "I can't read it properly. But, I can make out the date 1232 and something to do with a bishop and Richard. I thought he died in 1199?"

"A bishop?" said Holly, thoughtfully. "Yes! I know! I think it's referring to King Richard supposedly going to heaven. Apparently, because of his murderous sins, he wasn't allowed into heaven until the year, 1232. Which I think is just a load of old rubbish."

"So instead of those numbers referring to today at twelve-thirty-two, could they be something to do with the day he was killed and the year he supposedly went to heaven?" asked Jack, more confused than ever.

"So all this is just a waste of time?" wheezed BT, trying to help Martin onto his feet.

"Well, I've got something interesting..." said Martin, his hands on his sides still winded from landing on his back.

"No more of your silly games Martin!" snapped Jules. "Can't you see that I'm thinking?" she snarled, still looking at the plaque and muttering all the facts they had collated under her breath like some sort of super computer trying to process all the data.

"Well, alright then," huffed Martin. "It's just that I thought this looked exactly like the key we found."

"What do you mean it looks like the key? What does?" asked Holly, for the first time showing an interest in what Martin had to say.

Everyone apart from Jules gathered around Martin. "Well, it might not be much, but I thought that lamp up there looked like it was shaped like our key," said Martin, pointing to the ceiling directly above where he had been sprawled on his back.

Looking up Jack saw a black iron candle chandelier. In its centre was an outline about the same size and shape as his key. "Oh yeah," said Jack squinting upwards. "I see what you mean!" Rummaging through his pockets, he attempted to extract the key.

"See? I told you," beamed Martin.

"It's not here," announced Jack, frantically turning out all his pockets. He uncovered a train ticket, a scrap piece of paper, a couple of empty sweet wrappers, the smart business card from Roger Gante, half a blunt pencil, a packet of chewing gum and, nestled into the bottom of his pocket where it was now evolving into some alien life form, a mangy fruit pastel – but no ancient key!

Then he remembered giving it to Jules that previous night. "Jules, you've got it!" he exclaimed.

"Got what?" she said.

"The key! I gave it you last night."

"The key...? I'm sure I gave it you back," she muttered, more interested in trying to interpret the plaque than what Jack was saying to her about Martin's discovery.

"No you didn't," insisted Jack. "You asked to look at it when you were telling us about the date. Remember?"

"Yes," agreed Jules. "But then I passed it back to you. No, in fact, I gave it to BT, because he wanted to look at it as well," she recalled, now walking towards them and looking up to the ceiling to see what they all were staring at.

"Yeah," admitted BT. "But I gave it to Holly," he defended, quickly passing the buck like a hot potato.

"I don't remember having it," said Holly. "Oh, wait a minute!" he exclaimed, suddenly remembering. "Before I got chance to look at it, Martin snatched it from me," said Holly, relieved that he was not going to get the blame for losing it. All eyes turned accusingly on Martin.

"Erm," muttered Martin. "Yeah, well after I had it, I think I put it in the top drawer of Jack's bedside cabinet," he said sheepishly, fidgeting on the spot.

"Typical!" exclaimed Jack. "The one time we need it and you let us down."

"It wasn't my fault," protested Martin. "By then, you'd gone for a shower so I couldn't actually give it back to you. So I wanted to make sure I put it somewhere safe."

"When you've finished arguing, I think I've solved the

clue," said Jules.

Begrudgingly, Jack turned to hear what she had to say. Jules reckoned that the key needed placing into the medieval lamp. There was a window high up in the room and at twelve-thirty-two precisely, the light would flood through from the sun's rays, hitting the key at the perfect angle. The light would shine onto a specific spot in the room, which would lead them to the next clue. The accurate positioning of the chandelier meant that today would be the only day the sun would be at the right height at that particular time.

There was one slight problem with her theory: They did not have the key!

"I think, seeing as it's *his* fault, he should go back for it," smirked Holly, pointing straight at Martin.

"But I've hurt my back! And don't forget I twisted my ankle yesterday as well," said Martin, attempting to walk around in a circle with a limp while doubled over in two, just to prove his point. "Besides, Jack's the fastest runner."

Martin was right. Jack was the best chance they had. The longer they talked about it, the less time he would have to get to the hotel room, retrieve the key and return before the clock struck twelve-thirty-two. Time was running out.

***

Bending down, Jack placed his hands on his knees and inhaled sharply. Fortunately, their hotel was now only

216

one street away. Jogging around the last corner, Jack looked towards the hotel's front door. He could see the same car that had been parked there all night. The two policemen had not moved an inch. Sometimes grownups were so dense.

Cautiously, Jack jogged across the road keeping one eye on the car ensuring the policemen on watch did not spot him. By sheer fluke, a crowd of young school children on a fieldtrip offered him the perfect cover. Quickening his pace, Jack soon caught up to them. He would blend right in.

Jack noticed a man loitering outside the hotel. A nagging doubt in the bottom of his stomach told Jack something was odd. The man wore a long coat and seemed agitated as he paced up and down outside the main entrance to the hotel. Jack felt his heart almost explode inside his chest. The man was one of the Russian gangsters!

Chapter Twenty Five

Inconspicuously, Jack slipped through the group of school children and down the side street that led to the hotel's back entrance. As he raced through the hotel, he bumped into Mia. With a worried expression, she explained that a man had been querying Jack's whereabouts. Jack thanked her before scurrying off.

Cautiously he entered his hotel room, but there was no sign of his mum or Emma anywhere. He assumed – with his mum on the road to recovery – the two had probably nipped out to the shops. The key was exactly where Martin described, a miracle in itself was. Martin's ability to help on a scale of one to ten ranged anywhere between inept and pathetic!

Again Jack sneaked out of the hotel. Certain the coast was clear, he ran like the wind, running nonstop all the way back to the cathedral. He began to feel a stitch cutting into his side, but he had no time to worry about the sharp pain. At twelve-twenty-one, Jack ran across the large room where his friends were waiting – his feet echoing loudly on the stone floor.

"Shush!" hushed Jules. "We don't want to attract attention."

Doubled over and panting like a steam train, Jack kept his hands on his sides in an attempt to nullify the pain. Time was against them. Still wheezing, Jack feebly held out the key. They had a little over ten minutes.

A rustling noise caused Jack to glare at Holly.

"What?" said Holly, shoving his hand back into his crisp packet, a look of innocence painted across his face.

"You're making a racket...*from the packet*!" giggled Martin, laughing at his own clever rhyme as he fiddled with a brass orb on the rope barrier surrounding the king's tomb. Without warning, the orb twisting loose fell to the floor, clattering loudly across the hall. The noise was enough to wake a sleeping elephant. The scowl on Jules' face said it all. Martin ran to pick up the orb as it slowly rolled to a stop.

"We need to be quiet!" hissed Jules in exasperation.

A French man talking loudly caused Jack to look up. A tour party entered the room. Jule's plan was to stand on top of the tomb of King Richard and place the key in the metal chandelier hanging from the ceiling. That would be impossible now that a crowd of people were approaching. The guide slowly took the tour group through the room, stopping at every opportunity, until they were only a few feet away from where the children stood. By Jack's watch, the time was twelve-twenty-nine and fifteen, sixteen, seventeen seconds...

An Oriental looking man, wearing thick rimmed glasses and an expensive camera draped around his neck, kept raising his hand and asking the tour guide questions. The tour guide looked like he did not appreciate the countless interruptions, and neither did Jack. According to his digital watch the time was now twelve-thirty and nine seconds. He was now entering what officially was referred to as, 'panic mode'.

Jack caught sight of a cheeky grin on Martin's face followed by one of tourists muttering. Then the overeager man who had been asking all the questions, very quickly shuffled away. Martin had produced an SBD (silent but deadly). Within seconds, the last of the tourists disappeared out of sight in their attempts to vacate the room. Martin quickly clambered onto Holly's shoulders. "Right, you next," said Jules, pointing towards Jack.

The thought of climbing up past Martin's bottom did not appeal to Jack. But there was no time to argue. Slowly, he clambered up the human ladder, careful not to go anywhere near Martin's rear. Purely by accident, Jack kicked Martin's ear and stood on his nose as he was climbing. It was sweet justice. Swaying back and forth Jack stood on Martin's shoulders and raised the key towards the ancient chandelier. He was a foot short. "I can't reach it," he called out.

With only seconds remaining Jules scurried up the human ladder. "Ouch!" cried Martin. Jack felt Jules clambering up his back before heaving herself onto his shoulders. Struggling to keep his balance, Jack held out the key so Jules could grab it. Just as Jules had taken the key and climbed onto Jack's shoulders, he heard Holly complain. "That's disgusting!"

Jack sighed in disbelief. Of all the times imaginable,

Martin chose now to unleash another SBD, only this time Holly's face was directly underneath him.

"Hold still," Jules called. "I've nearly got it!"

"Hurry up!" shouted Jack. "There's no time."

The human totem pole began to sway violently. Struggling to support everyone after the Martin bomb, Holly could not support the human ladder any longer. Collapsing bodies tumbled everywhere.

"You idiot, Martin!" scolded Holly, blaming Martin for the collapse after letting off another SBD. "You're so uncouth!"

"Did you manage to do it?" asked Jack hopefully, believing deep down they had missed their one and only chance.

With a heavy heart, he glanced at his watch ... twelve-thirty-two and fifty seven seconds. It was all over. All their efforts for nothing. Another dead end.

Dancing across the room a ray of sunlight hit the key in the chandelier. A beam of green light fired from the key and shot across the room settling on the centre of a stained glass window.

"Look at that!" gasped Martin, still sat on the floor after the big collapse.

"Quick!" shouted Jack.

Jules, the first to react jumped up and dashed towards the light. On the stained glass window was a picture of a castle and a knight astride his white horse. Flowing across the window was an image of a pale blue river.

"Look! There's some sort of message hidden in the river," she explained. Pulling out a pen and piece of paper from her bag, she began hastily scribbling down the message.

The light soon vanished taking with it the secret message. It now just looked like an ordinary stained glass window again. "What did it say?" asked Jack, excitedly.

"Not too sure," replied Jules, staring at what she had scribbled down. "It's written in the same language as the note we found last year. We're going to have to get it translated."

What a huge let down. Jack was hoping the message would point to some sort of secret doorway, which would lead to treasure. Instead, all they got was a vague message in a foreign language that could take days, if not weeks to figure out. His dad was due to return that day. He might have arrived already. Then they would be off to Paris and then back home. The opportunity would be lost – maybe forever!

"Look!" shouted Martin, excitedly. "The light's now pointing at the coffin." A beam of light now shone down from the key.

"That's not a coffin," berated Holly. "It's a sarcophagus!"

"Martin's right," agreed BT, rushing from the stained glass window to the tomb of King Richard.

"Don't be silly. A coffin is made of wood and goes underground," explained Holly. None of his friends was listening to a word Holly was saying.

"It's pointing to that piece of stone jutting out," said

CHAPTER TWENTY FIVE

Jules. "NO, don't touch it, Martin...!"

Too late! Martin pressed the small stone nodule revealing a hidden compartment. Just as Jack was about to call Martin an unrepeatable name, a rolled up piece of parchment the size of a cigarette literally popped out from the opening. With lightning reflexes BT caught it cleanly in his hand.

"Hurry up!" urged Martin. "What does it say?"

"Hang on a minute. Give me time to look," replied BT, carefully examining the ancient piece of paper.

"I can hear footsteps. Someone's coming," urged Jack. "We still need to get the key back."

Without time to argue, the human ladder formed once more. This time, Martin was made to take the anchor position.

Retrieving the key without any further body crunching collapses, the group made its way back to the hotel. Not far from the hotel they passed an Internet cafe. Full of excitement, BT suggested translating the secret message they had found. After trying various translation websites, Jules finally found an interpretation she was happy with. "I think it reads...if you give me some room," she paused, trying to shove everyone back, with little success, as they pressed in around her. "The second corner lies in ruin."

"Doh! We already know that it's hidden somewhere in Rouen. That's why we're here," quipped Martin, trying to squeeze between Holly and Jack for a better view of the computer screen.

"No, you doughnut," said Jules. "Not Rouen – *ruin*!"

"And that's what I said," insisted Martin.

"R-U-I-N...as in crumbling castle type of ruin," Jules slowly spelled, letting out a huge sigh.

"But I don't get it. If the second corner was hidden in some old ruin back then, the building probably doesn't exist now. It would have crumbled away, deteriorated with the passing of time," said Martin.

"Another dead end," groaned Jack.

"There's something weird about it, though," continued Jules. "Those four letters in the very last word were each surrounded by a box. It could be a clue within a clue. I'm going to have to think hard about this one."

"Well, if you need time to think, then why don't we go back to the hotel and while we're at it, we could get something to eat," suggested Holly, at the same time his stomach let out a loud growl.

"Trust you, always thinking about your belly," laughed BT.

"But he does make a good point," Martin joined in. "And I'm starving too."

"Never mind food. What about the parchment we found in the Asparagus?"

"Sarcophagus," corrected Holly.

"That's what I said. Anyway, the point I was making is we might need to translate it while we're here, and we've not even looked at it yet," suggested Jack.

"Don't look now..." said Holly in a hushed voice, "but

I think we're being followed by one of those hooded weirdos. Martin, I said *don't* look!"

"Oops...sorry," said Martin.

"Quick, let's get back to the hotel. We can look at the parchment when we're safe, away from prying eyes," said Jack.

Arriving at the hotel without further incidents (that included Martin hurting himself again – in the last twenty-four-hours he had succeeded in twisting his ankle and landing on his back – twice!) they entered via the tradesmen's entrance undetected at the rear of the hotel. Unfortunately it meant trudging up the long and arduous stairs to the fourth floor. Martin chuntered all the way up the seventy-two steps about why they should have used the elevator.

Armed with new information regarding the next clue, Jack suddenly remembered the two Russians. He could not believe he had been so preoccupied that he had forgotten to tell his friends about them.

"David Tyrrell," said Jack aloud, as a flash of inspiration suddenly hit him.

"What about him?" Holly said.

"Well, don't you think it's a bit strange that the one person who was there when we discovered the last load of treasure just *happens* to conveniently be in Rouen when we're about to find some more?" asked Jack.

"What, David Tyrrell is here? In Rouen?" wondered Holly.

"Yeah, we saw him yesterday, snooping around at the hotel reception," said Jules casually.

"Well why didn't you tell me?" asked Holly, disbelievingly.

"Jack did! He told you earlier," replied Jules.

"Well I didn't hear him," sulked Holly.

As Holly skulked away from the conversation, Jack continued with his theory. "What if David Tyrrell is, in fact, George Martin?"

"How can he be, you dingbat?" scoffed Martin. "He's David Tyrrell."

"Yeah, but what if he's really George Martin in disguise? What better way to go undercover than to be a Police Inspector?"

"Like a double agent? That's cool," added BT.

"And the two Russians must work for him," elaborated Jack, with the whole plot slowly unravelling in his mind.

As they approached their hotel room, BT let out a gasp. Rushing forward, Jack took a closer look. A knife was stuck into the door of their hotel room. Not only that, a piece of paper was fastened down by the blade. With his body trembling, Jack leaned in closer and read the note out aloud...

Jack Hunter.
We have your mum.
We have your sister.
We have your rabbit.
Bring the second corner.
We meet 7:00 p.m. tonight in
front of the cathedral.
Make sure there's no funny
business ... if you want to
see them alive!

Chapter Twenty Six

"I can't believe they've got my mum," sobbed Jack, confused and dazed.

"I can't believe they've got my sister," said Holly, tears welling in the corner of his eyes.

"And they've got my little Lola," howled Jules. Completely absorbed by the tragedy she fell to the floor in a heap burying her head in her hands.

"Didn't you hear what the note said? They're blaming me," said Jack.

"And they think that Emma's your sister, too," added Martin gleefully. Then realising how upset everyone was, he slinked away and hid behind BT.

"What're we going to do?" pleaded Jack, in desperation.

"We need to give them the Second Corner," said BT, stating the obvious.

"I know that," said Jack, "but we haven't got it, have we? We don't know what it is, what it looks like, or even where to look."

"I remember seeing some strange markings cut into the stone down by the river, near where we crossed yesterday," said Jules, slowly getting back on her feet, her face all red and blotchy. "I'm sure it looked similar to that of the Four Corners."

"Finding that Corner is our only chance," said Jack. "We can't just turn up to the bad guys empty-handed and say, 'Sorry, we haven't got it.'"

"Jack's right!" For once Holly agreed with him. "If there's a chance we can find this Second Corner, then we have to try. Mum and Dad will never forgive me if something terrible happens to Emma. And to think, I've been so mean to her. I've been a real idiot."

Refuelled with adrenalin, Jack had no problem forcing his exhausted body towards the door that led back to the stairs. A mixture of worry over finding the Corner and the fear something bad might happen to his mum...

The more he dwelt on the events of the past few days, the more he realised how selfish he had been. All he needed to have done was hand the key over to Roger Gante. Simple! Let the professionals deal with it. Instead, it was all about Jack playing the hero again.

BT carefully removed a polythene bag from his rucksack, and using the cuff of his top, he pulled the knife and note from the door, gently placing them in the bag. Sealing it up, he dropped it into the front zipper of his backpack. "Evidence!"

It seemed an age before anyone could speak. "I think it's this way to the river," said Martin, as he hobbled along. The pain from his sprained ankle was clearly beginning to take effect.

"I'm sure it's that way," said Holly convincingly. "After all, I am a specialist in the field of history."

"And what's that got to do with anything?" asked Martin.

"History and geography are very similar subjects," he explained with an air of authority that Martin seemed to accept.

"Well, it's actually this way," said BT, disagreeing with both of them. He held his wrist in the air as though a UFO had fixed a tracker beam to his arm and was dragging him along. It turned out among the many amazing inventions and gadgets that he possessed, BT happened to have a water navigational attraction device built into his wrist watch! Soon after, they arrived at the riverbank.

"This way," said Jules, leading them towards the derelict buildings. Jack remembered seeing them the day before when they had been chased by the weird men in hooded robes. "Right, then...it was along here... somewhere. Yes!" she exclaimed. "Can you see the stretch of the riverbank that's edged with a stone wall?"

Although Jack thought Jules was talking gobbledygook, he did notice that a section of the river was much narrower than the rest. It appeared to be the same section of the river they had rowed across in the aerosol-spray-can-boat.

"Be on the lookout for a–"

"Found it!" Holly burst out, pointing to one of the stones making up part of the embankment. "Okay, try not to crowd around. You're blocking out the light," ordered Holly, crawling on his hands and knees trying to inspect the stone closely.

"What is it? What can you see?" said Martin, bobbing about like a fishing float, trying to get a better view.

"It's definitely the symbol of the Four Corners–"

"See? I told you," proclaimed Jules proudly, blowing on her fingernails and then polishing them on her top.

"Yes. Well done, Jules," said Holly through gritted teeth. "But apart from the symbol, there seems to be nothing else here."

Jack was deflated. There just *had* to be something more – his mum's life depended upon it.

"Can you push any part of it? You know, like we did on the gravestone back in Ghyll Church... Remember?" said Jules, desperate to get down and have a look for herself.

"No, no, I've tried all that. There's nothing else here... Hang on. Wait just a minute. There seems to be some sort of pointer – like an arrow." Jack watched Holly peer over the edge. "Yes!" exclaimed Holly excitedly. "There's a mark here. But I can't quite reach it," groaned Holly as he tried to look at it upside down, his head beginning to drain of colour. "Got it!" he shouted finally.

"What is it? Let me see. Let me see," chirped Martin.

"What looks like a keyhole has opened up," said Holly excitedly. "Jack, pass me that key you've got."

Jack hesitated. The last time he had given the key to one of his friends, they nearly lost it. "Hurry up, I haven't got all day," pressed Holly, raising his hand indicating for Jack to place the key in his palm.

Holly turned the key. Underfoot, the clunk of heavy machinery growled into life, causing the ground to vibrate. Then the oddest thing happened. A loud gushing sound came from the river. Jack turned to see a large barrier that stretched all the way across from one bank to the other rise up out of the water. "Look, there's another one!" whooped BT.

Two barriers separated a small section of the river. Before Jack was able to take in what he was witnessing, the water level between the barriers began to fall, just like Moses parting the Red Sea.

"It's like the locks on the canal," said Holly. Jack was also impressed by the sheer scale of the man-made ingenuity. The water quickly fell between the barriers revealing stone steps at their side of the embankment. The order of the Four Corners had hidden their secret – underneath the river.

"You're not going to believe this, but I've been thinking about the message we found in the cathedral. Those last words in the clue have been paining me. I don't think it says 'ruin' after all. I think it reads *Sein*. In other words, 'the Second Corner lies in Sein' as in the River Seine. I'm sure that's what it means. The clue hidden in the picture of the stained glass window was pointing us *into* the river. We might just find the Second Corner after all and, in the process, save Lola," explained Jules.

Jack knew what was coming next. If there was anywhere that looked creepy or uninviting, he could bet all the Beefeaters in London that would be where they would end up having to go. He watched Jules place a foot onto the first, slime covered step.

The South Tower

Chapter Twenty Seven

On the dry riverbed, fish flipped helplessly in tiny pools of water. An array of man-made objects lined the bottom of the river Seine. Jack gazed in astonishment at car tires, shopping trolleys, one Wellington boot, a small upturned boat covered in barnacles and even the remains of a rusty old car.

A strange sight smacked Jack right between the eyes. He could see – a door! On the far side of the river, a door was cut into the stone half way up the wall, hidden for centuries by the waters of the river Seine. Jack and his friends had uncovered a secret entrance. All they had to do was walk across the muddy riverbed and find out if the Second Corner lay hidden behind the door.

"No chance. I'm not going across there. It's filthy," complained Martin, as they reached the bottom of the slippery, slime covered steps.

Jack was inclined to agree with him. Not only had he been soaked, covered in stench, and then soaked through again, now he was expected to walk across the muddy riverbed that would surely suck them under like quicksand. "You must have some type of invention for that, eh BT? Have you got any more of that aeroSOLID stuff left?" asked Jack, hopefully.

"Sorry, mate. It was an experiment I'd been working on. The rest of the stuff's back home in my laboratory," replied BT.

"You mean your dad's old garage," laughed Martin.

Placing a foot on the riverbed, Jules shouted up to her friends. "It's not as muddy as you think. It's quite stony in parts. In fact I think it's actually a stone pathway."

"YUCK!" The cold wet mud squelched through Jack's trainers as he placed his foot onto the base of the riverbed. Soggy feet, again! It was becoming a habit.

Every time Jules passed a fish fighting for survival, she would pick it up and place it in a puddle, which meant it took twice as long as it should have to reach the other side, much to Jack's annoyance. He was anxious to find the Corner and rescue his mum. Eventually, they reached the secret door. The bottom of the door was level with Jack's shoulder. Holly raised his hands and pushed at it. The door was stuck fast.

"And how are we supposed to get in there?" asked Martin, flicking a piece of mud off the end of his nose. He was the only one in the group who had somehow managed to get mud everywhere, even on his face.

"Look, above the door," pointed BT, more interested in solving the clues than to be distracted by a mud-covered Martin. BT was right. Above the door sat seven square stones; each with a different letter carved into it. From where Jack was standing, it was difficult to tell what the letters said.

Jack decided now was a good time to look at the secret note from the tomb. He knew there had to be a connection. Fingers crossed, he quickly unravelled the parchment, hoping that somehow it contained a clue to unlocking the door that had been hidden for all those years underneath the river Seine.

There was a short message written in the centre of the parchment. Although it was clearly old, it was still legible. Jack was confused. He could read the message. It was written in very old English – but still English.

Under thee water yonder journey must
Beneath thee waves that hath not
From thee letters ye wilt
A wise man wilt select
Beyond thee door thine journey
Durst touch flame lest thee
Prithee disappear betwixt thee
Unto darkness dost cometh thine
Whither thou goest haste thee
Unto thee mere thou hast
Thee golden pyramid stand ye shalt
Find nary treasure, thee final

Jack blinked twice. It made no sense. Another dead end...

"The barriers...they're closing again!" shouted Martin, interrupting Jack's concentration.

Jack looked up at one of the wooden barriers. Water was trickling over the top. Martin was right. Seconds later, the river started pouring over the edge of the barrier. The channel was beginning to flood.

"What're we going to do?" panicked Martin, squealing like a pig.

"The letters from the clue," said Jules. "The last four letters were in boxes that actually look like those stones. I bet we need to press them in sequence...just like the last word in the message," she finished.

It all sounded good, but the puzzle was above the door and they were standing on the riverbed, stuck in the mud. Jack calculated, if they turned back now and made a run for it, they might just make it in time. To leave it any longer would be suicide. Unfortunately Jules had other ideas. "Martin, I need to stand on your shoulders."

"You're not standing on my shoulders! Your feet are proper filthy," he moaned, pointing at Jules' feet. Her trainers were sunk into the ground buried out of sight.

"We haven't time to–"

"Come here...I'll do it," offered Holly. Hastily he crouched down in front of the door allowing Jules to clamber on top of him. Time was running out. The channel was filling up quickly.

"It's not my fault. I hurt myself dinni...?" mouthed Martin to Jack, trying to defend his decision not to help. Jack flashed him a look of disbelief. "Honest. Remember when I slammed down on my back at the cathedral?" he pleaded, looking for sympathy.

The freezing water was already up to Jack's knees. They would never make it back to the steps in time. They were trapped.

BT started complaining how much he hated water. Jules was shouting at Holly to hold her still. Holly was complaining that Jules was getting heavy and Martin, well, he was just Martin. "STOPPIT! Stop messing about, will ya," shouted Jack.

His mum had been kidnapped. If he did not arrive with the Second Corner, he dared not think about the consequences. Jack was wound tighter than a coil. If only his friends would act serious – just for once.

Jules face was covered in muck and concentration as she deciphered the clue. Ignoring Jack's outburst she had already pushed three stones inwards but the fourth stone refused to move.

The water had risen to Jack's shoulders. Being the shortest BT was now struggling to stay above the water. He tilted his head back so his chin was pointing skywards as he tried to prevent himself swallowing any of the cold water.

As the river continued to rise, Jack turned in time to see BT disappear under the water. They were too late.

Chapter Twenty Eight

Standing on his tiptoes the water was already at Jack's bottom lip. He barely had enough strength left to hold BT's head above water. He could not last much longer.

"I've got it! I've managed to push the last stone..." shouted Jules, exhausted.

A flicker of hope set alight inside Jack.

He waited... and waited.

Nothing happened.

The water was inching its way up Jack's face. He closed his eyes. A vision of his mum appeared. A lump formed in his throat as he realised he was never going to see her again.

A clonking sound came from behind the door. Much to his relief, the door automatically swung open. Jules went tumbling through the open door. Holly quickly clambered after her. Martin helped Jack push BT up to Holly's outstretched arm. Just when Jack could not feel his toes and was ready to collapse with exhaustion, he also was yanked through the door.

All Jack wanted to do was rest, but the water was flooding in behind them. With a herculean effort, it took all five of them to push the door shut against the surging water. The door slammed with a bang. It was as though someone had placed a black hood over Jack's head. All light vanished.

Holly pulled his mobile phone from his pocket. In the fluorescent glow, Jack could make out the outline of his friends' faces. "I know there's one on here somewhere. Never had to use it before," muttered Holly. The phone was bleeping with each button he pressed. "There," he announced proudly.

A small beam of light, not even bright enough to compete with a match, shone out of his mobile phone. "What a waste of time," mumbled Jack, under his breath.

A bright light suddenly illuminated the whole room. Just as Jack was about to eat humble pie and acknowledge Holly's useful phone torch after all, he realised that the light was, in fact, coming from BT. "I know there's a couple more in here," explained BT, rummaging through his backpack, his face buried out of sight in his bag. "Here we go!" he said, tossing one to Jules and one to Jack. "It's a good job my bag is waterproof."

"What's it supposed to be?" asked Jack curiously.

"It's a glove torch," answered BT matter-of-factly – as though what he had given them was as common as a pair of socks. "You put them on your hand, press the button on top of your wrist and the gel crystals embedded in the palm emit a light beam whenever it senses you raising your hand."

"Cool! Where's mine?" asked Martin, excitedly.

"There aren't anymore," explained BT. "Sorry mate...I only had three." BT did not sound sorry at all. Jack imagined he had not given one to Martin on purpose. As a section of light shone across Martin's face, Jack noticed his bottom lip drop. "I thought because you'd hurt your back, you wouldn't want to be having to stretch your arms out all the time," BT added with a grin.

"Oh yeah," replied Martin, his voice sounding duller than dishwater.

"And what does this other button do underneath?" asked Jack excitedly, completely forgetting that he was soaked to the skin, trapped in a dark room, on a mission to find an unidentified object, and rescue his mum.

"Hopefully it blows you up," muttered Martin, sarcastically.

"I can't tell you," said BT, suddenly turning all serious. "But, whatever you do...don't press it!" he warned ominously. *Another reason not to give one to Martin,* thought Jack.

"Well, if you don't tell us, I'm gonna have to press it to find out. I, for one, don't want to be walking around with a radioactive bomb on my hand, do I?" said Jack.

"But you'll laugh," said BT bashfully.

"Go on, then. Tell us," Martin chipped in.

"It fires a kind of web-rope," explained BT.

"What do you mean, it fires a web-rope? You made gloves that fires webs just like Spiderman?" asked Holly, trying hard not to break into laughter.

"Yeah," admitted BT. "Look, I thought of the idea ages ago when I was younger whilst watching the film. Anyway, after I made them, I kinda thought it was a bit stupid, so I remodelled them using the gel crystals…"

"I think it's great," praised Jack. "How does it work?"

"Well, my dad made an extra strong batch of sticky ladders by mistake," BT explained. "Instead of remaining sticky, it sets rock hard like cement. My dad was stuck halfway up a wall for almost a full day until my mum finally came home from work and helped him down," reported BT. "So I used some of it on the end of a piece of elasto-rope I had lying around."

"Whoa, that sounds amazing. What's elasto-rope?" asked Jack.

"Here guys, look," shouted Jules, pointing to a pair of ancient torches attached to the wall opposite the entrance. BT pulled some matches from his bag. The torches sparked into life giving a better overall view of the room they were trapped in.

"I'm gonna have to get myself one of those bags!" said an impressed Holly. "It's got everything in it."

It turned out they were in a small chamber with a low roof. The only door in or out appeared to be the one protecting them from a million gallons of water. Jack felt like a lab rat trapped in a maze with no exit. When Martin made another one of his stupid remarks, the frustration of his mum's plight seized hold of him. Seeing red, Jack rushed at Martin, thrusting him backwards.

Martin howled, firstly in annoyance, but then in pain, as he was slammed into a wall. To everyone's surprise, before he could retaliate, the stone receded into the wall.

"There! Did you see that?" shouted Holly, pointing towards the wall in between the two amber burning torches.

"What?" groaned Martin, tired of being the butt of everyone's frustration. He was cold and wet too.

"When you knocked into the wall, I'm sure one of the torches moved," said Holly.

"I think you're cracking up as wel–" laughed BT.

"Hang on, yeah. I once watched a film where they turned the torches like handles and it opened up a secret door," cut in Martin, excitedly.

"Yeah, yeah, yeah...whatever..." mocked BT.

"No! I'm serious. Right?" protested Martin. "They turned one to the left and one to the right. But make sure you turn the right one clockwise and the left one anti-clockwise . Otherwise, a trap door will open up and you'll fall into a pit full of crocodiles. Look," he added, "I'll prove it to you." Everyone laughed. "What? It's true," insisted Martin.

"Don't let him touch anything! Every time he meddles with something, it ends up in disaster," warned Holly.

Peering closely at the right-hand torch, Jules noted excitedly. "You know what? It *does* look like it will turn."

"See...I told you," Martin stuck out his tongue and blew a raspberry in Holly's direction.

"Such a child," muttered Holly.

"It's worth a try. Anything's better than being trapped in here," admitted Jack, although he could not quite believe he was encouraging one of Martin's ideas.

"Make sure you turn the right torch first," repeated Martin.

Standing on her tiptoes, Jules heaved down on the burning torch. It slowly turned 90 degrees. At the same time, the flame extinguished. "See? What did I tell you?" cheered Martin, triumphantly.

"Well, I was the one who spotted them moving, don't forget," added Holly, rushing over to the other torch.

He turned the ancient torch, 90 degrees counter clockwise, just like Martin had suggested. The wall between the two torches began to rumble. Suddenly, a section of the wall began to disappear into the ceiling revealing a hidden opening.

Chapter Twenty Nine

A black hole beckoned. With reservation, Jack nervously stepped through the doorway, knowing it was their only option. The security of having his friends by his side gave him a confidence he did not possess. Jack stepped further forward flicking his hand and reactivating the crystal lights in his torch glove once again, the bright blue haze illuminating another empty chamber.

Jack had been in enough creepy underground corridors and chambers to realise he needed his wits about him. It must have been The Four Corners favourite hobby, laying booby traps. Jack wanted to be cautious, but the clock was ticking. Time was running out. Flashing his light around the room, Jack noticed a narrow archway. "Over here!" he called to his friends as he hurried towards it, casting fear aside.

The need to find 'the Second Corner' drove him onward. The ancient archway covered over by webs led to a stone staircase. At first the steps were inlaid with intricate mosaics, but as they descended deeper underground, the spiral steps became hewn from solid rock.

The steps went on and on, deeper and deeper until the stone walls were replaced by dry mud. The air around them grew cold and damp. The backs of Jack's calves were aching. "Finally!" cheered Jack as they reached the bottom.

They found themselves in a huge grand hall. Rows of solid stone pillars supported the ceiling. Giant statues lined one side of the long room, untouched by time. Cut from white marble, each impressive figure stood at least a hundred feet tall. Jack flashed his torch light causing the marble to shimmer, creating the illusion that the statues were actually moving.

"Why would someone go to all this trouble...and then hide them away down here?" puzzled Holly as he pointed the pathetic beam of light from his phone-torch in the direction of one of the statues.

"I bet this place used to belong to The Four Corners," said Jules, marvelling at one of the giant statues. "This one's wearing a crown...it's a giant King. I wonder who it's supposed to be and why they're hidden all the way down here?"

"Here, it looks like something's written at the base of the statue," exclaimed an excited Holly. "Yes, there is. There's some sort of symbol made up from a triangle, a couple of circles and what looks like a dagger running through it from top to bottom." With his finger, Holly drew an imaginary shape in midair just as he was describing it.

"Sounds more like a mouldy piece of cheese, if you ask me," grumbled Martin, still brooding over not having one of BT's torch gloves.

Aware that time was running out, Jack urged them

onward. They made their way past the royal statues between the pillars until they arrived at two arched doors as tall as a house. Cut from stone, the doors each had a round, giant handle at their centre. After a few minutes of shoving, heaving and pushing, Jack and his friends collapsed. The doors had not budged one single inch.

"Can I borrow your Spiderman glove, sis?" Martin begged Jules, tugging on her arm. Before she could say no, he pleaded, "Can I? Can I? Can I? Pleeeeeassse?"

"Oh, alright then," she conceded, reluctantly pulling off the glove and flinging it at him.

"Don't be pressing the bottom button," snapped BT. "Otherwise, you'll end up creating another accident."

"Don't worry. I'm not a baby, you know," replied Martin, stretching out his arm and firing beams of light everywhere. "Pew! Pew! Ka-pow!" he began shouting.

They were stuck outside the two solid doors with no way of opening them. "Will he ever grow up?" a frustrated Jack whispered to Jules, as they watched Martin playing at toy soldiers.

"Hey, guys, come here and look at this!" Martin suddenly whooped.

"It will probably be something useless," muttered Holly, unimpressed and disinterested.

"No! Honest..." protested Martin. "It looks like a secret coded entry pad!"

"He's right," confirmed BT, almost in disbelief.

"Let me see," commanded Jules, marching over. "Let

the professional in."

Everyone crowded around the spot Martin had pointed to. On the wall were square stone tiles that looked like an ancient puzzle. Symbols were carved into the tiles that looked like they were designed to move. Jack hoped with the right combination the door would open.

"I think it's just like one of those puzzle games I used to have when I was younger," said Jules, excited at the prospect of solving another puzzle. "You have these square tiles numbered one to fifteen in a plastic frame with one empty space. Then, what you have to do is move the numbered tiles around using the empty space until finally, you've got them all in the right numerical sequence."

"Coolio! I remember getting a mini-one in a box of cereal once with a picture on it," whooped Martin.

"But how are you supposed to know what order to put the symbols in? Unless they're Arabic letters that mean numbers and you just need to place them in order?" queried Jack, scratching his head in confusion.

Trying to spit his words out, Holly was jumping up and down in excitement behind Jack. "Th-the tri-angle," he said finally. After such build up, Jack had been expecting a bigger revelation.

"What? The one that looks like a piece of mouldy cheese?" asked Martin, busy shooting at the statues with his light beam.

"No, you morons, the symbol I saw at the base of the

first statue. Well, it's also on there," said Holly, pointing to the symbol on the puzzle. "So if we check out the other statues, we might find other symbols that will make up the combination. How many do you think we need, Jules?"

"Four, I think...erm...no, I'm positive! It's definitely four," she finally decided.

Quickly, they set about looking at the giant statues lined against the wall. "Got one," announced Martin proudly. "It's like a snake under a sun. I'm good, aren't I?" he finished before whizzing off to another statue to find the next symbol.

After what felt like hours, BT found the next clue, followed by Jack spotting the fourth and final symbol. Holly claimed to have found a secret entrance hidden behind one of the statues. Normally, Jack would have jumped at the chance to explore. A secret doorway had 'hidden treasure' written all over it. But, there was no time to investigate Holly's claims; they had just the small matter of a 'Corner' to find and his mum to save.

Ever since Jack laid eyes on the creepy man in the hotel foyer, everything made complete sense. He had never trusted the greasy Inspector Tyrrell from the day he first met him in his living room. The smarmy Tyrrell, sucking up to his mum and throwing around his charm – his act never fooled Jack.

"Can't you hurry up?" pleaded Jack, not wanting to be beaten by the man he despised. Time was a commodity they could not afford to fritter. Even if they did manage to find the prized Second Corner, there still the matter of exchanging it for his mum and Lola's safety.

Martin was hovering around, itching to touch the key pad. "Get your fingers off," snapped Jules, slapping his hand out of the way. "I'm nearly there...Yes! That should be right," she finished triumphantly.

Full of anticipation, the five of them stood back, pointing their torches at the large double doors, then back to the panel, and then over to Jules. They waited ... and waited ... and waited.

Nothing happened.

Chapter Thirty

"There's something written on these doors...maybe it's some sort of clue!" cheered Holly. As the others rushed over to see what Holly had found, he proceeded to read the words out aloud. "The writing's a bit faint, but it looks like:

Go
Flow
See
Carefully
Lie

and *Die* is the last word on the first door. Then on the second door it reads,

Wall
Call
Must
Trust
See
Key..."

He pointed the words out to his friends.

A flash of inspiration hit Jack. With trembling fingers from the excitement, he pulled out the old parchment revealed by the key back at the cathedral. "Wow, look at that!" he gasped. "The letter from King Richard's grave marries together with these letters to make another clue. Each word on the doors goes here, onto the end of each sentence. He carefully pieced it together with the letters they had just found and read:

So Under thee water yonder journey must, which you then add 'GO' and then so on.

So the next line says...

Beneath thee waves that hath not FLOW
From thee letters ye wilt SEE
A wise man wilt select CAREFULLY
Beyond thee door thine journey LIE
Durst touch flame lest thee DIE
Prithee disappear betwixt thee WALL
Unto darkness dost cometh thine CALL
Whither thou goest haste thee MUST
Unto thee mere thou hast TRUST
Thee golden pyramid stand ye shalt SEE
Find nary treasure thee final KEY.

See? They all fit perfectly!" exclaimed Jack, excitedly, as he scribbled them down onto the old parchment.

"The letters should tell us how to find the Second Corner," added Holly. He was so excited that he could barely contain himself. "We journeyed under the water, beneath the waves that did not flow."

"Yeah, because the barriers had stopped them," said Jack waving the ancient clue frantically in the air.

"Then it mentions the letters above the door that a wise man—"

"Ahem!" coughed Jules.

"Or *girl*... must select carefully," said BT, scowling at Jules for the interruption.

"And don't forget the flaming torch that I said was

a secret door handle," said Martin who had abruptly stopped playing around.

"Ahem!" Jules coughed again. "There's one vital point you're all missing," she continued. Jack knew she would be the one to spoil his important discovery. "Why would the final bit of the clue that's supposed to be telling us how to get here, already be down here?" she asked, logically. "It doesn't make sense."

"But that's just it," protested Jack. "Nothing does! Since when has any of this made any sense? Why can't this just be easy? It's so not fair! I just want to go home and be with my mum and dad."

Jack sat down and buried his face in his hands. They could not possibly have come so far only to find themselves at a dead end. This was their only way out. There was no way back. The door leading back to the river was no longer an option. Jack would never again see his mum or his dad. Although Jack's dad was the most annoying grownup Jack had ever had the displeasure of knowing, Jack still could not help loving him. Then there was his grandad whom he had only just recently met. It was all so unfair! Jack and his grandad had years of catching up to do.

The excited chatter stopped quicker than all the lights going out in a power outage. No one felt like talking.

Eventually, shattering the eerie silence, BT spoke up. "I think I heard something move over by the puzzle," he said, his voice echoing loudly.

"I hope it's not rats," gasped Martin, backing away.

"Do you always speak before you think? Since when do you see rats walking up walls?" said Jules, in exasperation. Jules moved closer to inspect the puzzle.

"Could be cockroaches then," added Martin, but his words fell on deaf ears. Jules discovered the front panel had receded into the wall revealing a stone tile.

"Let me see...?" said Martin, pointing a beam of light at the spot. "That's just a boring circle with four lines in it. Look it doesn't do anything," he said as he pushed the tile.

A loud noise echoed from the two immovable doors. Spinning around Martin raised his arm. The gel crystals burst into life again, just in time for the explorers to see the large doors begin to open.

"Who would have thought they would have electronic doors hundreds of years ago?" gasped Martin.

"They didn't," explained BT calmly. "My guess is it'll all work on some sort of winch and pulley mechanism."

Jack was no longer listening to BT's tedious technology lesson. Time was running out fast. He pressed the light button on his digital watch to see the time. The feeble green light barely illuminated the dial. It was nearly half-past-six, meaning only half an hour left to find the Corner, get to the cathedral, and save his mum.

"Quick!" he shouted, running towards the doors, which were now wide enough to drive a dumper truck through. "We haven't got much time."

He sped past the large doors without the slightest worry of what might lie beyond. There could have been giant spiders or a huge pit with sharks and crocodiles – even an army of statues suddenly brought to life after hundreds of years of hibernation. As it was, all he found were skeletons of human bodies strewn across the floor. Jack shivered.

"Where's all the treasure?" asked Martin, unimpressed by the very large and extremely empty chamber.

"Never mind the treasure, we need to find the Second Corner," advised Jack, who was busy scouring the room for clues.

"You've got to admit that it does seem a bit weird, don't it...going to all this trouble of building this massive underground palace, then put nothing in it...don't you think?" asked BT.

Hundreds of different symbols were painted all over the walls. An assortment of chipped and broken earthenware pots were piled up in a corner of the room. At the back of the room, a tall wooden staircase disappeared high into the roof of the tall chamber. Jack did not need to worry anymore about how they were going to get out, although the rickety staircase looked like falling apart and disintegrating into a thousand pieces at any moment.

"Maybe we're supposed to look for the wheel symbol with the cross running through it. I'm not too sure, but I think it's going to be somewhere on these walls," said Jules with a calculated assurance.

Jack did not know what to think. They had fought their way through countless medieval traps and puzzles just to end up in an empty room. What's more, the secret message that they'd found was even more baffling now that they had figured it out!

A stone shelf high up the wall ran all the way around the room. Holly was adamant it was a trough full of oil intended for lighting the room. He convinced BT to throw his last few matches where he was pointing. Jack stood back as a fire sparked into life. Flames quickly licked their way around the massive chamber. They could now clearly see every detail in the room.

"I have to admit that was pretty nifty, Holly!" said Jules, paying her rival a very rare compliment.

"I've seen it!" cheered Holly, suddenly pointing high up one of the walls. His smirk was so wide it would take a week to wipe it from his face. Although Jack hated not being the one who solved the puzzle or found everything, he would be happy just to discover what the bad guys were after and rescue his mum.

A valid point suddenly dawned on Jack. "That's all well and good, but how are we going to get up there?" His friends fell thoughtfully silent at his clever, although unwelcome observation.

"Martin, I need that glove back," said BT interrupting everyone's thoughts as they tried to find a way of getting up the wall to where the symbol was painted. Even if they made another human ladder like they had done in the cathedral, they still would not be tall enough.

"What...? Why mine? Why not Jack's?" moaned Martin. After everyone gave him a cold stare, Martin peeled his new toy from his hand and tossed it begrudgingly to BT.

"Stand back, everyone!" announced BT, pulling on the second glove and striding closer to the wall. "Whatever you do, don't try this at home..." he warned his friends. "I've had lots of practice."

At that, he reached for the second button...

Chapter Thirty One

A web-like rope coated in the extra strong sticky ladders shot out of BT's wrist instantly attaching to the wall. Jack could only watch in disbelief as BT ran and leapt at the wall. Grabbing hold of the rope, BT hauled himself up the wall.

"What now?" called BT, reaching the symbol in record fast time.

Jules was the first to speak. "Try pressing on the picture!" Turning to Jack, she added. "I don't think it will be anything elaborate. The very fact they hid the symbol so high up the wall was a challenge in itself."

"Will do..." BT called out cheerfully.

Jack strained to see what was happening. The silence was killing him. Just as he was about to check his watch again, BT shouted.

"Hang on a mo...something's happening. It's like a secret drawer...and I think... Yes! There's something inside it."

BT swung back down rejoining Jack and his friends.

"That was the coolest thing I've ever seen!" praised Martin, slapping BT on the back. "I was wondering... can I—"

"No, you can't," said Jules sternly, second guessing that Martin's next question was going to be, 'Can I have a go?'

"What did I say wrong?" said Martin, innocently shrugging his shoulders.

Leaving the two Brown kids to argue, BT proudly showed off his find, before passing it to Jack who examined it closely in the light. It appeared identical to the one he already possessed in every detail, even down to one of the corners tipped with gold.

"Isn't that almost the same as the one we found in the secret tunnel last year?" asked Holly.

"Exactly the same," agreed Jack. "But if this is the Second Corner, then does that mean the one we've given Danny to keep in his safe is, the *First* Corner?"

Tired of arguing with her brother, Jules took a renewed interest in the ancient artefact. "I wonder what's so important about this, anyway?" she mused, taking the triangle from Jack and spinning it around between her fingers.

"It doesn't really matter, does it? We need to get this back to save my mum," replied Jack as Jules handed the triangle back to him.

"And don't forget my sister," added Holly.

"And my Lola," Jules reminded them.

"Are you sure climbing up those steps is the only way out?" interrupted Jack, totally disinterested in what Jules had to say about her rabbit.

"Well, if you can find a better way..." said Jules, heading in the direction of the rickety staircase. "But time's running out!" She looked pointedly at her watch.

"Yeah! Come on Jack, you wuss. It's not as if there's going to be a six-hundred-year-old elevator lying around, just in case some wimp happens to stumble across this secret chamber," mocked Holly, bouncing up and down on the wooden staircase, as if to prove a point that it was safe.

Jack stood at the bottom of the wooden steps. Looking to the top of the rickety staircase made him feel dizzy. Just as he was about to place his foot on the first step, Jack was certain he saw something shiny glinting in the dust under the fragile stairs. Bending down, Jack carefully swept years of settled dust aside and plucked the glistening object from the ground.

Jack stared at the small misshaped item. He was holding a very old, gold coin. "Hurry up!" shouted Jules. His friends were already weaving their way up the medieval stairs. With time against him he needed to hurry.

The Second Corner safely in his grasp, Jack began the long arduous climb up the stairs. There must have been hundreds of steps. The further he climbed, the more Jack's feet grew heavier and heavier. Sweat streamed down his face.

Somehow, he managed to urge himself onwards. He could not believe how silly he was acting over climbing a few steps. With each step he took he kept telling himself they weren't that high.

Ahead Jack watched as his friends stepped off the staircase and disappeared into a gap in the wall. Eager to follow and get off the ancient staircase, Jack felt a fresh burst of energy. He climbed the final rise of wooden stairs in record time. Stepping from a wooden platform at the top of the stairs, he entered into a stone corridor. Leaning against the wall, he needed to take a deep breath before wiping his sweaty brow with his sleeve.

His friends were nowhere to be seen. Although he figured they were only too glad to get out and into the fresh air, he was still gutted they hadn't waited for him. After following the windy corridor for a few minutes, he spotted a dim light. Turning a corner he found a few stone steps that led upwards through the ceiling – the way out. A welcoming light flooded the corridor. As he scrambled towards the stone steps leading out of the underground chamber, a loud noise stopped him dead.

BANG! BANG!

The deafening sound ricocheted around him. Gunshots! Treading cautiously, Jack climbed the last couple of steps. Lifting his head just above a stone ledge, he anxiously peered around. To his surprise, he could not see his friends anywhere. He was inside a large, but very old looking basement and he was standing in the middle of a stone coffin.

An eerily familiar voice caused his body to freeze with fear.

"Jack...Jack Hunter? Come here... quickly!" it commanded.

It was David Tyrell!

Chapter Thirty Two

Jack wanted to run back to the hotel and hide inside the bed. If he pulled the duvet over his head and shut his eyes long enough, maybe just maybe, the nightmare would disappear. His natural urge was to escape, but the knowledge that his friends, his family, and even Jules' pet rabbit were all in danger gave him an inner strength. He rose, stepping nervously out of the tomb, still clutching the treasured Corner. "Quick, Jack! Over here," David Tyrrell called.

Instinctively, Jack spun around desperately looking for reassurance his friends were unhurt. They were nowhere to be seen. Then he noticed something on the ground that looked out of place. A body lay still on the stone floor. The evil fraudster had shot one of his friends.

A lump grew in Jack's throat. He wanted to run.

Something did not add up! Then it dawned on him. The body was not only far too big to be any of his friends, but dressed in completely different clothes. None of his friends wore big brown boots.

"Jack! Don't listen to him. It's a trap," a voice came from the other side of the room. Inspector Roger Gante of Interpol was positioned behind a wall near the entrance.

"No, Jack! Don't trust him. Quickly! Come to me," implored David Tyrrell.

Jack looked up and saw the Inspector beckoning him. His head throbbed from the mental confusion. Then, he noticed David Tyrrell was holding something in his hand – a revolver!

Jack's legs began shaking.

Slowly, he backed away from David Tyrrell. Why had he travelled all the way from Barnoldswick? The police Inspector suddenly shouted at Jack, "No! Don't...!"

Nearly tripping over his feet, Jack made a run for it. As he ran past the fallen body, Jack recognised the dead man as one of the Russians from the ship. He must have been one of Tyrrell's henchmen. Fortunately, Interpol had been on hand to save the day.

One more step and he would be safe.

"Ohhh, Inspector," Jack half gasped, half sobbed, falling into the safety of Roger Gante's arms. "Where's my mum and my friends?" he gasped. "Are they safe?" Tears burning his cheeks.

"Yes, yes," the Inspector assured him somewhat distractedly. "Now, have you got it?" he asked, roughly yanking at Jack's wrist. "Where's the Corner?"

Jack was confused. A thousand questions raced through his mind. Roger Gante's grip tightened around his wrist. "Have you got the Corner?" demanded Roger Gante, less patiently this time.

"Yes, but I-I, you...?" stumbled Jack, full of confusion. "I don't understand–"

"I gave you more credit than that," laughed Roger

Gante, no longer polite or charming. The Inspector's trademark flouncy words were now replaced by a deep gravelly voice. He ripped the ancient triangle from Jack's grasp.

"Come out with your hands up...we have you surrounded!"

"One false move and the boy gets it," yelled Gante across the room.

Nothing made any sense. *Where were his friends ... his mum ... the rabbit?*

The harder Jack tried to pull away from Gante's clutches, the tighter the man squeezed his wrists. "Come on, we haven't got much time," barked Roger Gante as he made for the doorway, dragging Jack with him up an old stone, spiral staircase. Jack was forcibly pulled across the inside of an old church, between the wooden pews, making it to the door just as Inspector Tyrrell shouted after them.

Outside, a car with blacked-out windows sat waiting, engine purring in readiness. Without mercy, Roger Gante, who in Jack's eyes was no longer worthy of the important sounding M.I., dragged him out through the door and bundled him into the back of the car.

"Drive," Roger ordered the man sat behind the wheel.

Just before they pulled away, Jack caught a glimpse of the driver's face. He instantly recognised him as the other Russian from the boat. Jack was sure he heard a bullet ricochet against the car's rear window.

"Okay, George," the driver replied.

"George? I thought your name was Roger," asked Jack, innocently.

Turning to face him, Roger Gante's piercing eyes cut right through Jack. "Roger...no, no, no, although it was a nice touch, don't you think? I'm George Martin," he cackled.

"*You're* Geo-orge Martin? The one everyone's after?" said Jack, his confusion swallowing all other emotions.

"The one and the same," said George, a crooked smile livening up his dour face. George turned around and picked up his prize.

Jack could see George was distracted, mesmerised by the beauty of the golden-tipped triangle. "What's so special about that anyway?" asked Jack. His body ached from pain, but his desire for answers burned deeper.

"This," laughed the man, "is one of the Four Corners. Once we have all four in our possession, we shall rise again and claim what is rightfully ours."

The car slammed to a sudden stop and Jack fell forwards banging his head on the headrest. He wanted to reach out and stop himself from the impact, but his hands had been bound together behind his back. Then the car door swung open and Jack was ordered out of the car.

They were parked alongside the river Seine. Jack could see a white speedboat moored at the end of a wooden gangway. Roger Gante or was it George Martin ... Jack was confused … appeared to have every base covered, everything planned to the finest detail.

"What do you need me for?" pleaded Jack, desperate to see his friends and be reunited with his family. "You've got what you came for."

"Insurance," growled George.

Jumping into the boat George fired the throaty engine into life. Jack felt a rough hand pushing him from behind. The Russian shoved Jack into the boat causing him to tumble forwards. Catching his shoulder on a tool box as he fell, Jack yelped in pain. "Quick, the rope," George ordered the Russian lingering on the jetty. The minute the man obeyed George's orders and threw the rope off its moorings and onto the back of the speedboat, George pushed down hard on the throttle. The boat sped into action.

"Boss? Boss?" Jack faintly heard the man call out over the roar of the boat's engine. Leaving his own accomplice behind, it was becoming apparent that George was a monster who showed no mercy. And to think, when they first met, he had given Jack a whole fifty Euros!

While George kept his eye on what lay ahead, Jack had a brainwave. The tool box!

Awkwardly using both of his tightly-bound wrists, he tried opening the lid of the toolbox. Luck was with him, it was unlocked! A hacksaw was the first thing he laid eyes on and quick as a flash, he awkwardly set about cutting through the rope. The feeble rope was no match for the sharp teeth of the fresh blade. It cut his fetters like a hot knife slicing through butter. In no time at all the rope fell away.

A piece of wood lay at the side of the toolbox. A flash of reckless inspiration gave Jack a crazy notion. Taking the length of wood, Jack attempted to sneak up behind the master criminal and hit him on the head. His stupid plan might have actually worked if a beer can had not been rolling across the middle of the deck. Jack accidentally kicked the can that rattled along the deck, inches away from George Martin. George turned around just as Jack raised the piece of wood.

The next thing Jack remembered was landing hard on his backside with a throbbing nose. He spied his weapon lying a few feet away. George marched straight towards where he lay in pain. George was too quick for Jack, kicking the piece of wood further from him.

"Do you really think you can take this away from me?" laughed George, waving the treasured Corner. Grabbing Jack by the scruff of his neck, George lifted him up until they were eye to eye.

What had *he* been thinking? *It never happened like this in the movies*, groaned Jack. He must have been crazy.

With an iron-like grip, George was squeezing the life out of Jack. His feet dangling helplessly in mid-air Jack suddenly remembered the glove torch. With every ounce of strength remaining, he slowly raised his arm and opened his palm. A bright gleaming light shone straight into the criminal's evil eyes temporarily blinding him.

George let go of Jack and stumbled backwards clutching his face. It was the reprieve Jack needed. Without stopping for a moment to think through his ludicrous plan, Jack rolled over, grabbing the piece of timber, before jumping to his feet and hitting George Martin on the side of his head.

Dropping the Corner from his grasp, the man staggered backwards, his eyes boring straight through Jack.

Did I hit him hard enough? Jack wondered, *or did I just poke a stick into a wasp's nest, making things ten times worse?*

Then, like a tall tree at the mercy of a lumberjack's axe, George crashed backwards.

The boat lurched forward. Catching Jack off guard, he tumbled backwards. The unconscious criminal had inadvertently fallen onto the throttle, sending the boat hurtling across the river at full speed.

A bridge lay directly in front of them. The boat was on collision course. Bouncing over a squall, the unmanned speedboat changed direction, narrowly missing the bridge stanchion. Out of control, the boat sped under the bridge.

Jack could now see a motorboat at the other side of the bridge lying directly in their path. He needed to get to the boat's controls – fast! Staggering back to his feet, Jack surged forward. The speedboat was going too fast. He wasn't going to make it. The two boats were going to crash.

Chapter Thirty Three

Determined to catch George Martin and save Jack Inspector Tyrrell began barking out orders. Dozens of police cars arrived simultaneously on the bridge. Jumping from the safety of their police car and dashing into the middle of the chaos, Martin, Jules, Holly, and BT's only concern was for Jack's well being. "Get back here!" screamed the Inspector.

Jack's friends ran to the edge of the bridge, peering through the railings. They could only watch in horror as the speedboat raced straight towards the motorboat.

"Jack, no!" shouted Jules, shrugging off the attempts of a police officer to pull her away from the edge.

BOOM!

Orange flames leapt into the sky followed by plumes of black smoke. The four British school children fell silent. Martin chewed his lip. BT felt tears trickle down his cheeks. Holly bowed his head.

"Jack!" sobbed Jules, turning to the nearest of her friends, Holly, and throwing her arms around him.

Road blocks were already being set up as more police arrived at the tragic scene.

"Urgh!"

"What did you say?" demanded BT, pushing Martin hard in the chest for being insensitive considering the circumstances.

"Say what?" defended Martin. "What's your problem?"

"Hel-urgh," a faint voice called again. BT looked at Martin and Martin looked at BT before realising neither of them was making the funny noises. "Help!" they heard, only a little louder this time.

Hurriedly they looked over the side of the bridge. Swinging by his wrist from a length of web-rope was an almost unrecognisable twelve-year-old boy, face covered in black ash. Jack had still been wearing BT's glove. Jack was alive!

"H-hurry up," he stammered between breaths. "I-I can't han-ng on much long-ger."

Two policemen rushed to aid the boys. After hauling Jack over the railings to safety he collapsed at their feet.

A gun shot fired, then another. Panic followed. Dozens of police officers scurried for cover. Crouched ... arms raised ... pistols ready.

The sound of a badly-tuned engine came within ear shot. With what little strength he had left, Jack looked fearfully across the bridge. A ghastly yellow minibus spluttered into view. It was his dad. How embarrassing!

The police blockade at the far end of the bridge allowed Roger Hunter to drive through. To Jack's surprise, his dad and Grandad were not the only passengers. The minibus came to a standstill, the door opened and Emma emerged, Lola securely tucked in her arms. Emma ran towards Jules, who, to his relief had stopped hugging a rather crimson Holly.

When Jack saw his mum climb out the passenger door, he somehow found the strength to get up from behind the police car and run towards her. "Mum! Mum! You're safe!" he called out, relieved.

"Of course, you silly boy," she said, giving him a big hug. "Why wouldn't I be?"

"Because the bad guys kidnapped you," he sobbed.

"What're you talking about?" said his mum, surprised. "Your dad arrived in Rouen this morning, so we decided to go out for the day, seeing as I was feeling better and *you*, you were supposed to be visiting the cathedral for your homework. I left a note for you on your bed explaining everything, just in case we were later back than we expected," his mum said, clearly not amused as she realised the war zone around them was a direct result of her son's handy work. "Look at all the chaos you've caused!"

"But I didn't–" defended Jack.

"I can't leave you alone for five minutes," she continued, as she looked over the edge of the bridge at the boat still ablaze. "The very shame of it." His mum turned away, shaking her head.

"Now then, you little rascal," his grandad called.

Before Jack could fret over whether he was in for another scolding, his grandad broke into a smile and gave him a great big bear hug. Jack felt his back crack, but he didn't complain. He was happy to see his grandad again, and happy his dad was there (the yellow-peril minibus included), happy his friends were with him and happy his mum was safe and sound.

His dad gave Jack a playful jab in the ribs. Thankfully, a hand tapped Jack on the shoulder, saving him from the embarrassment of an interrogation, or worse still, his dad calling him Jacky.

"Can I have a word with you, young Hunter?" asked Inspector Tyrrell. "Did George Martin give you anything?" Jack looked at him blankly, not quite sure what he was referring to "...anything at all?"

Jack placed his hand in his pocket and pulled out the fancy business card. After looking at the name Roger Gante M.I. one last time, he handed it over to the Inspector.

"Mmm, very clever, don't you think?" asked Tyrrell.

Unsure what he was referring to, Jack simply nodded in agreement.

"One of the most wanted criminals posing as someone from Interpol, right under our very noses! And to think, his identity was there for all to see..."

"Wher-what do you mean?" stuttered Jack.

"I mean," said the Inspector, "that his name was there all along! See?" Jack still did not know what Inspector Tyrrell was babbling on about. "Roger Gante M.I. If you rearrange the letters, I believe you arrive at George Martin. It's an anagram. Rather ingenious if you ask me! Don't you think?"

Not wanting to be beaten, Jack tried shuffling the

letters around in his own mind. When the Inspector realised Jack still did not follow, he added. "Too many crosswords I guess."

The man dropped the plastic card on the ground, stamping on it with his regulation police shoe. Bending down, Inspector Tyrrell picked up the broken card. "Just as I suspected," he muttered to himself. Pulling out a small round metallic object that had been hidden inside the card, he waved it in front of Jack's face. "There you go, lad. What do you reckon to that?" asked Tyrrell.

"I don't know," shrugged Jack, bemused at what the Inspector was showing him.

"It's a bug. As long as you carried this around with you, George Martin would know exactly where you were at all times."

"So that's what was causing the interference with my sneaker phone," said BT as he approached. "No wonder it made all those woo-wah noises!"

Now everything made perfect sense, and yet no sense at all. Jack just wanted to get some sleep.

***

The last two days in France were uneventful. Brimming with excitement, Jack had been looking forward to talking to his friends about their amazing time but, Jack's parents, determined not to let anything else happen to the children, watched over them like hawks, never letting them out of their sight for as much as a nanosecond.

His mum and dad even arranged for Grandad to sleep

close by Jack and his friends to make sure they were safe. Well, that is what they claimed, although Jack figured it was so they could make sure he and his friends couldn't get up to anymore mischief. This meant they never got a single opportunity to talk about their recent adventures.

During the evenings, Jack's grandad would keep him and his friends occupied with his amazing stories of his sea adventures. Fancying the idea of becoming a sailor when he was older, Jack pictured himself captain of the fastest ship and vanquishing pirates. But the best story of all was the one his grandad told about discovering buried treasure when he was a boy.

His grandad would talk without stopping to yawn or give any indication that he was tired. There was a real burning fire of excitement in the old man's eyes that somehow drew you into his stories. The details were so vivid that Jack could almost imagine he was there too.

It wasn't until the ferry home that an opportunity arose for Jack and his friends to talk. His grandad, an ever present night owl, finally nodded off. He was out cold with three day's' worth of sleep to catch up on. Roger Hunter was out walking around the decks getting some fresh air. (His dad would not admit it, but Jack knew he was feeling seasick.) His mum had gone off with Emma, leaving Jack and his four best friends together, alone.

"So Roger Gante M.I. was actually George Martin. If you mix up the letters they're the same name," explained Jack, knocking Holly's hand away from the last jam doughnut. "You've already had two," he scolded. "That's mine and I'm saving it for later."

"So, if George Martin was the world's number one public enemy and the two Russians were working for him, where does that opera singer fit into all this?" asked Martin, sporting a white sugar moustache with deep red jam covered lips.

"Not only that, but George let slip that he was actually part of The Four Corners–"

"Elizabeth Coldaire is not an opera singer. She's an actress," interrupted Jules.

After a heated debate, they decided that Elizabeth Coldaire was not one of the bad guys, but was trying to keep the key hidden from the Four Corners. No one had a clue who the strange robed characters were supposed to be. Holly's theory was that, whenever you have an ancient society trying to take over the world, there was always another group trying to stop them. "So, in other words," he recapped in his usual droll historian-know-it-all voice, "if The Four Corners society is still operating today and is after those hidden Corners, then it makes total sense someone else is trying to stop them. It's just a pity that the Second Corner blew up on that boat. Otherwise, we would have two of them, meaning we'd be halfway to discovering the greatest treasure the world has ever known," said Holly, wistfully.

"But that's the point I don't understand..." moaned Martin.

"Keep up, will you," laughed BT. "The bad guys are after the hidden treasure so they can take over the world. Just think of it as a James Bond movie."

"Ohhhh!" Realisation lit up Martin's face. "Coolio! Well why didn't Holly just say that in the first place?"

"So do you think there are more of them Corners?" asked Jack, a smile spreading across his face.

"Could be. I reckon once you've got all four and put them together, the combined symbols will most likely tell you where all the treasure is hidden," speculated Holly.

"Talking of gold, how come there was no treasure hidden in that underground chamber? It seems crazy to go to all that bother to make an amazing place like that, but then have nothing down there. I mean that ceiling must have been a hundred feet high," said BT, standing on tiptoes and raising his hand as high as he could to reinforce his point.

"Behind the secret door...you know that door I found hidden behind the third statue on the right?" explained Holly.

Before anyone could reply or go into more details, the handle began to rattle on their cabin door and in stepped Roger Hunter, cutting their conversation dead.

Half an hour later the ferry was docking at Dover. The adventure was almost over. They climbed aboard the giant lemon, his father firing it into life before driving the minibus off the ferry. As they drove down the ramp touching down onto English soil, a tinge of regret, a realisation that the holiday and the adventure were finally over, washed over Jack.

"By gumdrops, it's raining," announced his grandad.

Looking out of the window, Jack got a shock. A bright light flashed, temporarily blinding him. A hub of noise and activity suddenly surrounded them. "What's going on?" he asked bemused. The docks was crawling with reporters and camera crew.

"My guess is, Elizabeth Coldaire," said Jules.

"What? Elizabeth Coldaire was on our ferry and I missed her? Why you didn't tell me?" swooned Roger Hunter. "What rotten luck!"

"Jack! Jack!"

Jack turned and looked out of the window in time to see a throng of reporters surging towards their bus.

"Jack Hunter?" an older man with a pointy goatee and wearing a trilby hat rapped on the glass next to where Jack was sitting. "Is it true that you defeated George Martin?"

"Did you help break up the world's most wanted criminal ring?" asked a pretty girl reporter.

"Any chance of a smile for the Daily Galatica?" requested a third. Another bright light flashed through the window. Jack temporarily shielded his eyes.

"What's it like to be famous?" asked another.

"You're a hero!"

"They'll make a movie about you!"

"Can we have an interview?"

The superlatives were being fired at him from all angles. Jack's brain barely had enough time to file the words, let alone process or respond.

"Don't stop, Roger! Keep driving," he heard his mum shout.

A gunshot rang out across the docks, causing all the reporters and camera crew to duck and scatter.

Accustomed to the ancient vehicle's temperamental nature none of the passengers aboard the ghastly yellow minibus flinched. Thick smoke bellowed out behind the minibus – a backfire. Jack would never live it down. How embarrassing!

***

The minibus finally passed the road sign; *Welcome to Barnoldswick.* They were only five minutes from home. The adventure was over. Tomorrow they would be back at school.

"We're gonna have to go back to France," said Jack.

"No chance, mate. There's no way I'm going back there," said Martin waving his hands furiously. "Everyone is crazy."

"What on earth would you want to go back there for?" whispered Jules, trying not to wake Lola who was peacefully sleeping on her lap.

"Because we never did get to Disneyland...did we?" noted Jack. At that, all his friends burst out laughing.

Although Jack had originally wanted desperately to go

to the theme park, secretly, he would not have changed their week's adventure for all the fun rides in the world.

The Garden

Chapter Thirty Four

Jack sent a crunching blow slamming down on his clock as the alarm went off for the third time. School! He could not believe the school holidays were over so quickly. It was almost as if he had been on a rollercoaster ride of high octane, adrenalin-fuelled excitement – and yet he hadn't even been on a single ride.

Flicking his lamp on and rubbing his eyes, Jack slowly crawled out of bed. Still trying to remove a stubborn piece of sleep from the corner of his eye, Jack stumbled across to the window and poked his head through the curtains. The sky was grey and dull. It wasn't raining, which surprised Jack, because it always seemed to rain in the north of England.

As Jack was contemplating the merits of a nice long hot shower versus spending an extra ten minutes back in bed, a garish pink and leopard print coloured limo drove into view. The longest car he had ever seen – almost the length of a bus – crawled along his street at five miles per hour.

Before he could panic, the car drove past his house. Relief! He could not cope with any more out-of-the-ordinary experiences. The stretch limo stopped in the middle of his street. Jack watched as it then proceeded to back up, reversing into the empty space outside his house.

Jack needed to stop being paranoid every time he saw something unusual. The passengers of the luxury car must be visiting the neighbours. The car door opened. Jack held his breath. He watched in horror as a man in a long robe stepped out. For a split-second, he froze with fear. The robed man looked in Jack's direction. He quickly ducked below the window.

Sitting on his bedroom floor underneath the window, his back against the wall, Jack waited, unsure what to do. All he wanted was a normal life.

"Jack, darling?" his mum called. "Can you please come downstairs? You have a visitor."

Jack did not know what to do next. He searched frantically around the room in the hope that a solution would miraculously jump out of thin air. He was just about to ring Jules for her opinion when he remembered he didn't have his phone. His dad had confiscated it the previous night, just because apparently he had been, the words his dad used, 'cheeky' and 'lippy'. As much as Jack pleaded his innocence his dad did not listen. So unfair!

Just when all seemed lost, Jack spotted his walkie-talkie. In one fluid movement, he dove across the room, grabbing the walkie-talkie from the set of drawers, before bouncing over the other side of his bed. Crouching safely behind his bed, Jack turned it on.

"Come in BT...over?" he whispered as though the robed man was standing outside his bedroom door.

Other than the crackling of the walkie-talkie, silence

replied.

"Jack? Did you hear me? Can you please hurry up?" He could hear an irate edge in his mum's voice.

There was nothing to it. Without his friend's advice, there was no alternative but to escape through the bedroom window. Breaking the world speed-dressing record, he threw on his school clothes. Jack slung his backpack over his shoulder and hurriedly drew back the curtains.

His plan seemed a good idea at first, but when he looked out of the window, the front lawn appeared a long way down. Jack was no chicken. With gritted teeth, he slid open the window. Not for the first time that morning, Jack ducked down out of sight. The robed man was still there. *Who then could be his unannounced visitor?* He wondered.

Before figuring out his next move, his mum knocked on his bedroom door. "Jack? Jack? Are you decent? I'm coming in."

"I-er-you-c-can't," he stuttered. Before he could finish his sentence, the bedroom door swung open and in stepped his mum. She looked unusually flustered.

"What are you doing down there? Did you not hear me?" she barked.

"Uh! I-er-I," he stammered.

Oddly, his mum seemed excited. "We have a special guest, Jack. I still can't get over it. And I haven't even done my make-up," she flustered. "Your dad will not believe this. Why didn't you tell me?"

Unable to comprehend a single word his mum was saying, Jack slowly dragged himself towards his bedroom door. If he did not know any better, he would think she sounded goofy.

His escape route blocked by his mum, Jack had no alternative but to face whoever was visiting. Begrudgingly, he followed his mum down the stairs and into the living room where a surprise awaited him. There, sitting on the sofa in a matching pink leopard print hat and coat, was the world-famous movie star, Elizabeth Coldaire.

Elizabeth Coldaire? In his house!! Jack stood dumbfounded.

"Hello again...Jack, isn't it?" she spoke softly.

Jack was still in a state of shock. Before he could think of what to say, his mum reappeared with one of her best china cups and placed it on the oval coffee table. "Erm, I just need to go and get ready, madam," said Jack's mum. Bowing politely, she edged backwards out of the room. His mum was acting like a star-struck teenage groupie. Jack was so embarrassed.

"So...you took my key and unlocked the secret?" asked Elizabeth Coldaire.

"I-erm-I–" stammered Jack, still unsure of the reasons behind the movie stars impromptu arrival.

"It's okay," she interrupted. "I'm not cross – quite pleased, in fact. You see, if you and your friends hadn't been so clever and courageous, then I fear the Corner would have fallen into the wrong hands." Elizabeth Coldaire then paused while she removed both pink satin gloves and proceeded to pick up the china cup and saucer. Still wondering why she was at his house, Jack could only stare as she took a sip before placing the cup down on the coffee table. A replica of her lips in bright pink now decorated the edge of the china cup. "You still have the key, don't you?" she asked.

Jack simply nodded.

"Would you be a saint and fetch it for me?" she asked, her voice sounding sweeter than honey.

Jack was out of his seat, up the stairs and into his bedroom before Elizabeth Coldaire had a chance to draw breath. Seconds later, Jack was handing over the ancient key and the actress' handkerchief he had picked up after their first, chance encounter.

The more Jack thought about things, the more something did not fit right! Jack scratched his head, hoping that would help. On this occasion, it did! *If the robed man waiting outside was one of the bad guys, did that mean Elizabeth Coldaire was working with George Martin?* Now he was even more confused.

"Do you mind if I ask you a question please?" Jack boldly asked.

"Well I guess that all depends…"

Jack was not sure whether she meant yes or no, but he still asked his question anyway. "If you're not working with George Martin, then what are you? Erm, I don't mean literally, what are you..." he could feel his cheeks burning as he floundered. "What I meant to say, erm, I can't think of the words. You know what I mean...do you? I just don't really understand?"

Silence fell as Elizabeth Coldaire took another sip of tea. Finally, she replied. "Ah, I see. I'm afraid I can't elaborate too much, but suffice to say, I'm not one of the Four Corners."

"But how come this coin I found was down there. My friend, Holly, said it's supposed to be Alexander the Great, which makes it well old. Which means a big pile of treasure was there and then moved, doesn't it?" Jack looked at her longingly.

The famous movie star leaned forward and continued in a hushed tone. "Your friend is very perceptive. I'm afraid I'm going to have to take the coin..." Elizabeth Coldaire had already put her gloves back on. She held out her pink leopard print covered hand. Nothing made any sense to Jack. After deliberating for a moment, he placed the coin in her hand. "Now try and steer clear from all this or you'll only end up causing more trouble. Boys your age should be playing sports and computer games or whatever it is you do. At least the Second Corner has now been destroyed, everything is magnifique...!"

She gave Jack an ice-cold stare. He felt a shiver run through his body and he shrank back into his seat.

"I won-wondered," spluttered Jack, thinking about telling her she was wrong and that two Corners were in his possession. Unbeknown to anyone else, Jack had rescued the Second Corner from the boat literally seconds before it blew up. "Oh no, it doesn't matter," he decided quickly.

"Well, the reason I came here, besides collecting the key, of course, was to let you know that for your own protection, we will be keeping an eye on you. And please, no more crazy adventures. You've caused enough chaos as it is."

Again, Jack felt his cheeks begin to burn.

***

After checking his watch for the thirteenth time in less than a minute, Jack was finally resolved to the fact he was officially late. After quietly opening the school door, he checked right and then left. The coast was clear.

As he took another step forward, a voice bellowed along the corridor. "HUNTER?!"

Jack gasped.

Holding a mug of tea, Mr. McIntyre stomped towards him with a beaming face. "I hope you've got a good reason for being late," grinned the sulky teacher. Of all the rotten luck, Mr. McIntyre just happened to step out of the staffroom at that precise moment.

SMASH!

Mr. McIntyre dropped his mug. A flood of tea ran over Jack's shoes. "E-liz-a-bet-hhh Col-ddd-aire?" said the shocked teacher, licking his palm and frantically smoothing down his hair at the sight of the world-famous movie star standing behind Jack.

"Yes, sir..." Jack boldly replied. "I do have a very good reason for being late!"

THE END... or is it?

Did you solve the Ottendorf cipher?

If so, visit **www.martinkingauthor.com** to open the secret passageway. Then discover the location of the treasure room to uncover a hidden chapter and complete this story.

At the end of the hidden chapter will also be a code breaker to help you solve the puzzle below and unlock the secret to book three...

JACK HUNTER
Legend of the Two Giants

66-15-2
16-2-59
66-97
54-4-3-97-31-16
66-15-2
31-97-11-4-2-11-65
65-2-31-11-2-66
9-65
15-2-3-10
33-9-66-15-9-4
66-15-2
8-9-13-4-66-65
16-2-59

Lightning Source UK Ltd.
Milton Keynes UK
UKOW050619300113

205590UK00001B/3/P